A NEW SE

The Liaison Officer was a slug.

It floated in a glass tank, blowing frothy green bubbles as it spoke. The voice that came through the speakers was a wet, slobbery gurgle.

Yake Singh Browne, Assistant Liaison Officer with the One Hundred and Thirteenth Interstellar Mission, listened politely.

"My people have nowhere invested as much time in the nature of your species as you deserve," the slug-thing said. "Yet, despite your odorous appearance, we look forward to eating and enslaving you—and we apologize if we are presumptuous."

Yake cleared his throat uncomfortably. What was the damn slug driving at anyway? This was going to require some fancy tap dancing . . .

Avon Books are available at special quantity discounts for bulk
purchases for sales promotions, premiums, fund raising or educa-
tional use. Special books, or book excerpts, can also be created to
fit specific needs.

For details write or telephone the office of the Director of Special
Markets, Avon Books, Dept. FP, 105 Madison Avenue, New York,
New York 10016, 212-481-5653.

CHESS WITH A DRAGON

DAVID GERROLD

MILLENNIUM

A BYRON PREISS BOOK

AVON BOOKS ◆ NEW YORK

For Dennis and Mark,
with love

AVON BOOKS
A division of
The Hearst Corporation
105 Madison Avenue
New York, New York 10016

Book design based on hardcover book design by Alex Jay/Studio J
Logo design by Lebbeus Woods
Book edited by David M. Harris
Millennium Books and the Millennium symbol are trademarks of Byron Preiss Visual Publications, Inc.
Special thanks to Richard Curtis

First Avon Books Printing: November 1988

TABLE OF CONTENTS

A
GAME
OF
NESTLINGS

K!rikkl polished its mandibles slowly while it considered the layout of the game board. There was much too much at stake, and there were far too many unanswered questions. Perhaps it had been a mistake to accept this invitation.

For instance, how many eggs were in the Dead Mother's egg pouch—and what kind? K!rikkl knew there had to be at least three fat Xlygit larvae and a Knrkt—G!ligglix's aggressive betting was proof enough of that—but if there weren't any host-grubs, then the pouch was valueless. To K!rikkl anyway. Complicating the matter was the fact that G!ligglix already claimed to have a whole family of host-grubs in its nest; but as far as K!rikkl could tell, G!ligglix did not yet have a Knrkt. But then again, maybe G!ligglix didn't want one. A Knrkt could be its own worst enemy.

"!" said K!rikkl in quiet annoyance. This was not working out at all well.

"??" questioned Hnaxx, turning a multi-faceted eye in K!rikkl's direction.

"A remark of annoyance, my dear host. You may perhaps be far too good a player for my skills. This game promises to last long into the night."

"Should the game last that long, my dear guest, it will be a grand testimony to your own skill."

"If we do not starve to death first," agreed K!rikkl.

G!ligglix giggled. "I think you overestimate *all* of our abilities. . . ."

K!rikkl ignored the remark. G!ligglix was a fat, rude, grossly distended, gluttonous, ill-mannered, profiteering liar. G!ligglix was also quite rich—which was why K!rikkl had considered joining the game at all. Now, K!rikkl was beginning to discover just how G!ligglix had gotten so rich. As a result, K!rikkl's goals for the evening were beginning to

3

shift. The young Ki!lakken had initially thought to play for brooding-advantage; now it seemed more cautious simply to play for quiet survival.

K!rikkl clicked again and considered the possibilities.

In order to complete its own nest and close the Blue Cycle with a breeding, it would have needed to find host-grubs elsewhere on the playing field. That no longer seemed possible. All the host-grubs had either been eaten or claimed. Without grubs, K!rikkl's only hope of survival to the Dawn Cycle would be through neutering—and that was *always* a bad idea.

Hm. Perhaps it could barter a single grub from Hnaxx. Although it wasn't an official rule, the way the game was generally played, the host was honor-bound to succor a needy guest—except all of Hnaxx's grubs had already been impregnated. And now, Hnaxx was studying K!rikkl's discomfort with a wry amusement.

That left only Hnaxx's young broodling, Rrr. A very unlikely possibility, K!rikkl decided. Rrr was already too close to the honor of Gracing the Table. There was very little possibility of Rrr giving advantage to anyone else—at least not unless there was also significant gain to Rrr's own nest.

The question was—what was in Rrr's nest?

Hmm.

No, that wouldn't work. There was nothing to be gained by lending an advantage to Rrr. Besides, Rrr was young and tender. There was a lot of juice and protein in that exoskeleton. K!rikkl wasn't the only Ki! who'd noticed the plump tenderness of the youngest player. By unspoken agreement of the more experienced players, Rrr had already been selected as the guest of honor for the banquet later this evening.

No. Definitely no. Rrr was not the solution to K!rikkl's problem on the playing board. Indeed, if K!rikkl aided Rrr, it might very well find itself the target of the other players' enmity—and the cautious Ki! knew where that led. K!rikkl had no intention of taking Rrr's place on the table of Hnaxx the Munificent.

Hmm. And hmm again.

K!rikkl arched its large, green, triangular head forward and made soft clicking noises in its throat. It bent itself low and gave a tremendous performance of studying the board, blinking and peering and tapping at the pieces with ferocious deliberation.

Yes.

There was no other way.

K!rikkl made a decision.

It sat back on its haunches and growled low in its throat. A sign of annoyance and frustration.

"A cough, perhaps?" inquired Hnaxx politely.

"Yes, perhaps," replied K!rikkl noncommittally. The whole thing stank of a trap. The seven other players—distant members of Hnaxx's nest—waited courteously while K!rikkl polished its mandibles. Finally, with deliberate grace and elegance, K!rikkl withdrew a blue silk scarf from its sleeve and laid it across the game board.

One of the other players made a sound of disgust with its hind rasps. Rrr backed away from the board in silent relief. G!ligglix clacked impatiently. "A suspension, K!rikkl?"

"Unfortunately, dear G!ligg, one must attend to the needs of the physical world before one can achieve the spiritual."

K!rikkl inclined its head to each of the players in turn. "I invite you to refresh yourselves as well, so that we need not be interrupted again." The Ki! smiled and straightened itself and stepped back away from the low dais of the game field.

As it stepped toward the door, K!rikkl clacked a warning syllable to the host-grub it used as a burden-beast; the pale-pink creature gabbled back a nonsense syllable of its own from where it squatted in the corner. The thing was almost as fat and naked as a larva—and it was getting embarrassingly large as well. K!rikkl would have to plant eggs in the grub soon or someone might begin asking the wrong kind of questions.

Keeping its features impassive, the Ki! moved with a quick, high-stepping gait; it bowed through the gossamer curtains of the pavilion and out into the night. The low building behind it glowed with muted blue warmth.

The others complained, but they tossed their egg-pouches

onto the table and followed. Protocol demanded that no Ki! stay unattended in the room with the board and the other players' pouches. Throwing a silk therefore had only limited strategic value in the overall structure of the game. It worked against the other players' balance much more than it worked against their positions. Nevertheless—an experienced player could take advantage of even the smallest possibilities. . . .

K!rikkl was neither hungry nor thirsty; nor did its bowels need emptying. Nor did it need to lay an egg. K!rikkl did not need to polish its carapace, nor did it need to groom its foreclaws or even empty its parasite pouch—but there were other needs, much more important, so K!rikkl began to take care of all of its intimate physical functions anyway.

The Ki! stepped haughtily across the carefully manicured lawn to the lush grove of dormant Fn^rr and began digging a trench for its excreta. K!rikkl dug slowly and patiently, scraping its hindclaws through the soft dark earth with the utmost of care. It was still several months until the spring, when the Fn^rr would begin walking and talking again. This far south, the Fn^rr spent almost as much of the year rooting themselves as they spent being ambulatory—but the Fn^rr were only dormant, not unconscious. They often remembered the events that occurred during their dream-time; many of the Ki! hoped that the care that they took in fertilizing the roots of the Fn^rr would be remembered and rewarded in the summer.

At least that was the justification for being so thorough and meticulous.

K!rikkl filled the trench with a jet of oily fluid and then pushed the dirt gently and precisely back over it. Then it paused to polish its foreclaws carefully with a soft silken cloth before it turned back to its companions.

K!rikkl knew that it couldn't delay the procedure of the game for too long, or that would surely arouse the questions of the others; but nonetheless it paused to sniff and chew a small bundle of herbs before turning back to the pavilion. It offered the herbs to the others, but they politely declined. K!rikkl waved its foreclaws in amusement and clacked its mandibles in gaudy appreciation. The sound echoed loudly across the lawn. "Well," K!rikkl trilled loudly to Hnaxx and the others. "Shall we play?"

The host-grub was still sitting in the corner; it paid no attention as the Ki! stepped back into the pavilion. It was grooming or playing with or examining the soft flesh of its body—probably looking for fleas. K!rikkl clacked at it; the creature looked up and gabbled back, then resumed its abstracted examination of itself. K!rikkl snicked in annoyance and then turned its attention back to the board, lifting the silk scarf and considering the possibilities again.

K!rikkl waited until all the others had resumed their positions, then blinked and tapped and hesitated—and made the move it had already decided to make long before it threw the scarf, a move so deliberately neutral it suggested that K!rikkl had decided not to breed at all for the next six cycles of the game. K!rikkl glanced over at the grub in the corner. It was counting the toes of its left hind foot.

Hmm.

Perhaps there were breeding possibilities with Rrr, after all. Not just here in the game, but beyond its boundaries as well. If Rrr survived, K!rikkl might—*just might*—indenture the Ki! as a mate. But . . . if Rrr were to survive the evening, then who might take its place? Hnaxx? (Too bony. And besides, it was considered bad manners to eat the host, no matter how bad a player it was.) Lggn'nk? (Maybe. But Lggn'nk seemed greasy and unappetizing.) Dxxrt? (Possibly. But Dxxrt was too cautious a player to be trapped.) G!ligglix would be ideal, of course . . . all that juicy fat—

The grub had ceased its examination of its foot and was now picking parasites out of the dark folds of its crotch.

So! G!ligglix did have a Knrkt after all! That meant that its aggressive betting was only a bluff to encourage the other players to extend themselves too soon! What a marvelous trap G!ligglix was laying. If it succeeded, it could turn loose a very hungry Knrkt on the egg pouches of all of the other players and guarantee itself a permanent breeding advantage.

K!rikkl kept its face impassive. If G!ligglix could be forced to keep its egg pouch sealed until the Knrkt awoke—

and Knrkts always woke up hungry—G!ligglix could be eaten out of the game and onto the table before even the first generation was ambulatory! Hmm. And hmm again. What an absolutely delicious possibility. . . .

But it would have to be very carefully managed. Either Rrr or Hnaxx would have to come into enough of a fortune to shift the balance of trading; the breeding negotiations could not be opened while there were still incomplete trades. If the close of barter could be delayed through three more rotations—no, that would be too obvious. Besides, Hnaxx was already befortuned; it would have to be Rrr—but any advantage shifted to Rrr would have to be done anonymously. Perhaps on the next scramble—or better yet, the one after that; but it was going to be very tricky to arrange. An advantage should not be used to betray itself—especially not this advantage.

This was going to require some study.

If the other players ever found out just how thoroughly trained the fat, pink host-grub really was, it would not be long thereafter that K!rikkl would be the guest of honor at a stinging. Or worse. K!rikkl might find itself hosting grubs of its own.

K!rikkl rasped its hind legs together in a loud, absent-minded whirr. G!ligglix looked up curiously; the others continued to study the markers on the inlaid board.

"Your pardon, dear G!ligg," said K!rikkl, lowering its eyes shyly. "I was just considering a most interesting possibility."

G!ligglix's reply was noncommittal.

THE
SMILE
AND
THE
SLIME

The Liaison Officer was a slug.

It floated in a glass tank, blowing frothy green bubbles as it spoke. The voice that came through the speakers was a wet, slobbery gurgle.

Yake Singh Browne, Assistant Liaison Officer with the One Hundred and Thirteenth Interstellar Mission, listened politely to the soft whispering of the translator in his ear without expression. The Dhrooughleem were so painfully polite, it was depressing. There were at least sixty-three ritual courtesies to every Dhrooughleem transaction.

Yake stood quietly with his hands at his sides, waiting for the Dhrooughleem to finish. The slug-thing in the tank was finally concluding the blessing of Browne's genetic lineage, his parents, his egg-cluster siblings, his mating-triad, his territorial governance, and the noble egg-clusters he had already—or perhaps would soon—sire upon his brothers in the pond. The translators weren't sure. Or perhaps the concept was untranslatable because there was no human equivalent. In any case, it made for some fascinating daydreams.

The Dhrooughleem Liaison finished its recitation and waited without expression for Yake's response. Keeping his face carefully blank (a smile was considered an insult to a slug; the showing of one's teeth implied that one was thinking of the other as a possible meal), Yake began to thank the Dhroo Liaison profusely. His thanks went on for several moments; it wasn't exactly a formal part of the ritual, but it was an expected one.

When Yake finally finished, the Dhrooughleem burbled something green. The translator whispered: ''Unfortunately, as pleasant-garble as it is to acknowledge each other—garble-

11

garble, tree shrews taste terrible—occasionally we must pause
to garble-garble our respective purposes as well.''

Yake agreed. He turned around to the desk beside him and
picked up a folder of documents. ''You have been so helpful
to us, *Mn Dhrooughlorh,* that I hesitate to ask new imposi-
tions of you, and yet—it seems that there is still much my
people do not understand. There are many more subjects
about which we would like to experience clarification. I have
taken the trouble of preparing a list—'' He held it out to the
Liaison's mechanical manipulators.

The Dhrooughleem made no move to take the folder.
''May I respectfully garble-garble a new subject, *Mr.
Browne?*'' it asked.

Yake tried to hide his surprise. ''I beg your pardon?'' In
eight hundred and twelve previous meetings with the
Dhrooughleem, the subjects covered had been so meticu-
lously according to ritual that the meetings could have been
scripted in advance. This was a total break in protocol—

''—must abase myself with a thousand salt water apologies for garbling the pattern of grace and [pneumatic gill
slits] and [soft red mud] which we have so carefully wrought
together—''

Yake struggled to keep his face impassive. He hoped that
the proctors were getting all this. Indeed, they should already
be ringing for the Ambassador.

''—may I have your permission to garble a concern?''

Yake felt uncomfortable. The translating circuits were
having greater than usual difficulty with the Dhrooughleem
inflections. Clearly, something was not right. ''Yes, of
course, *Mn Dhrooughlorh,*'' he said. ''Please continue to
garble—I mean, share your circumstance.''

''My people have nowhere invested as much time in the
garbling of the nature of your species as you deserve—[??]
[Despite your odorous appearance, we look forward to eating
and enslaving you] [??]—and we apologize if we are garbling
presumptuous, of course—but have we been uncareful in
explaining the nature of our service here?''

''No, of course not,'' Yake was quick to reassure. ''The
Dhrooughleem have been extraordinarily helpful to us in our

missions. Were it not for the Dhrooughleem, we would not be able to query the InterChange nearly as efficiently as we have been.''

"Yes, that is precisely the issue, dear garble." The Dhrooughleem writhed in its tank, stirring the brackish-looking water into murky brown and green swirls. "We are concerned about your relationship with the Exchange. [Your egg clusters are a lovely shade of ignorance.] Perhaps we do not understand you well enough. Perhaps you do not understand us—''

"Oh, no—we understand you perfectly!'' Yake caught himself in mid-word, and corrected himself hastily: "I mean, we understand you as well as we can. That is, allowing for cultural and biological differences and the inefficiencies of our translating circuits.''

"Yes, that is the [offspring]! Perhaps we have failed to garble what your responsibilities are to the membership of the Exchange.''

Yake cleared his throat uncomfortably. What was the damn slug driving at anyway? This was going to require some fancy tap dancing. "As I understand it, *Mn Dhrooughlorh*,'' Yake began carefully, "the InterChange is a gathering of many different species from many different worlds. Admission is granted to any species that can maintain a mission here. Is that correct so far?''

"Unfortunately so. You are aware also of the responsibilities and [fresh excrement] that such membership entails?''

"Information requested must be paid for with information of equal value—or by services. My species understands the concept of value exchange quite well.''

"That is the concern and [antique chair collection] of my species. I am relieved to hear you say that. I had so feared that we might be [enamored] about the circumstances, Mr. Browne.''

Yake was about to reassure the Dhrooughleem again when something went *twang* in the back of his mind. He said, instead, "As we understand the contract, new species are allowed a period of indebtedness in which to acquaint themselves with the . . . the rules of the game. Have we been mistaken about that?''

"Again, your grasp of the [slime mold] is admirable, Mr. Browne. It is I who must wear the [seasoning-spices] of embarrassment. Please to accept a thousand and three apologies for even raising the subject. The question was brought up only as a [traffic ornament] of our great respect for your species, and our concern that your [enslavement] be applied most deliciously.''

"I beg your pardon? What was that about 'enslavement'?'' (Yake promised himself an appointment with the Chief of Translation Services. This was intolerable!)

The slug burbled a blue froth. "[I have exercised my hair.] What word didn't you understand?''

"The word for 'service,' I believe.''

The slug blew a single red bubble. A bad sign that. The translator whispered: "I said nothing about service.''

Yake sighed and retreated into the safest of rituals. "Pardon my ignorance, *Mn Dhrooughlorh*, but I am confused here. I abase myself at my own stupidity. Please do not feel that the misunderstanding is a result of any of your words or actions. Please accept my apology for any inference that you have done less than your best. Perhaps in my eagerness to ease your discomfort at having to travel and meet in such a cumbersome device as a tank on wheels, I presume familiarities that I should not.''

Yake reached up and twiddled his hair with his fingers, the closest he could come to an abasement wriggle. He felt like Stan Laurel doing it; then, having satisfied the ritual, he continued carefully. "Somehow, I get the feeling that there is a subject we are discussing about which I do not have all the facts. May I request that you speak your concern a bit more directly? I promise you that there can be no offense taken here. We are searching only for the clarity of truth within your information.''

"Since you ask for candor, I can only give it to you.'' The slug sank back down in its tank. Its eyes—all eight of them—were suddenly very large and very black. "My species is quite concerned about the size of your information debt.''

''We have asked for something we should not have?''

''No, no—it is not the current package of requests that is the issue. It is the extremely large amount of information that you have already [ingested]. The interest is accruing perhaps a bit more rapidly than you are aware? Indeed, at the current rate of accrual, you are going to strike your debt limit in less than eighteen of your months. My species is [be-fargled] that your species will be indentured before you have had an opportunity to present a [vat of boiling chemicals] to the Monitors.

''It is clear to me, of course, now that you have reassured me here, that you and your species fully understand the nature of the circumstances and are not without knowledge of the [edibles]—but of course, the cleverness of your species is such that you must already have a [foundation garment] to present to the InterChange, and I have been dreadfully out of line for even garbling the subject. Please, no offense is meant—''

''—and none is taken.''

''However, the [garlic seasoning] of this discussion was to let you know that the Dhrooughleem stand ready to continue to assist the Terran Mission in any way possible—''

''We thank you for that.''

''—and if your [menu of green flavors] is turned down by the Monitors, we stand ready to assume the indenture of your entire species—''

''I beg your pardon? It sounded like you said 'indenture—' ''

''—We have assumed many indentures, and always at the worst equable rate. We would take great [condiments] to be the kindest of guardians while your [enslavement] is [ingested]. You promise to be a most [delicious] species.''

Yake felt dizzy. The translator hadn't been out of focus at all! Oh, dear Lord in Heaven!

''We have hesitated to mention this, of course, out of our fear that we might somehow [gringle] your [pentacles]. To

some species, even to imply [malodorous deflation] might be
smelled as a [sphincter] of offense. It [tickles our bladders]
that you [descendants of tree shrews] are so [happy to be
eaten]. Some species would see such a [bereavement] as a
[dishonorable suicide]. It is our very high regard for you
[things that belong on a plate] that mandates our concern
here. If you would pass this [offer of ingestion] on to your
own superiors so that they may be aware of our concern and
our willingness to purchase your indenture and [eat your
livers], we would be most—''

The rest of the interview was a blur.

THE
TEETH
OF
THE
SLUG

The Crying Room looked like a war zone.

Every terminal was alive, whether someone was sitting before it or not; every screen was either scrolling through long columns of text or flashing brightly colored three-dimensional graphs and translation matrices. The diplomacy technicians were moving quickly from work station to work station, pulling reports from one, giving instructions to another, keying in new instructions to a third. The Section Chiefs were clustered in small groups at or near the big briefing table; that end of the hall was raised above the rest so that most of the large screens at the opposite end of the chamber would be visible from that position. The table itself was covered with a six-hour detritus of half-empty coffee mugs, still-glowing clipboards, scratch pads, pens, crumpled wads of paper, and red-bordered printouts of classified documents.

Secretaries of all four sexes moved quietly around the edges of the room, gathering up the debris of previous confrontations and handing out weaponry for the next. Orderlies and robots worked to replenish sandwiches and keep the coffee urns full. In one of the corners, a thirty-year veteran was quietly weeping in a chair.

The initial shock of realization had not yet sunk in. The diplomatic staff was still trying to assimilate the scope of the problem. The damage reports were still coming in; and the damage was not only worse than anyone had expected, it was even worse than they had feared.

The Crisis Management Team was not even waiting for the full report; they had already moved into the second stage of the job—fixing the blame. The sound level was horrendous; the cacophony was on its way to a record decibel level. The accusations, denials, explanations, excuses, justifications, rationalizations, and reasons stormed and raged back and forth across the room like a caged tornado, carrying in their fury a blizzard of notes and images, documents, diagrams, photographs and papers. The conflicting evidences of blame and blamelessness flickered and flashed across the wall of screens until all meaning was leached from even the simplest of facts. The situation assimilation process had long since aborted and collapsed in a state of information implosion.

The Ambassador from Terra had once been known for his Million-Light-Year stare. Now his eyes were veiled and gray. His stare was focused on the cold cup of coffee in his hands, and it was impossible to tell what he was thinking. A jabber of voices swirled around him, but apparently he was listening to none of them.

Yake Singh Browne sat quietly at the opposite corner of the table, making meaningless notes on a pad of paper while the arguments continued. He did not even look up when the chair flew past his back. Two career diplomats had already had to be pried apart by their colleagues and sent to opposite corners of the room.

"Sir? Sir—" someone from Analysis was trying to attract the Ambassador's attention. Yake glanced across the table and began to wonder if the Ambassador was crumbling under the strain. The Old Man looked dreadful. The Assistant Secretary of Something-Or-Other was jabbering insistently: "I hate to say 'I told you so,' but we've been advocating fiscal responsibility for decades, and no one's been listening to us. This is precisely the kind of debt position that we've been warning against—"

"It's really the fault of the Library Department," said the bulldozer-shaped woman on the other side of the Ambassador. "You know how those hackers are. They see something interesting on the menu, they automatically download it with the idea of exploring it in detail later. Of course, they never do. Something more interesting always comes along. We have material in our banks that we won't be getting to for a hundred years! And as far as assimilation goes—"

"Really, I reject that!" came the angry reply from halfway down the table. "If we'd had the help we'd originally asked for, that material wouldn't be going unread. I say that if we'd *had* the librarians, we could have catalogued the material already. There's probably a hundred different answers to this situation already in our banks. We just don't know where to find them—"

"I think you're all missing the point here. You've been played for fools by the Dah—D'haroo—Dhrooughleem." That was Madja Poparov, the new Policy Supervisor from the InterChange-Council Advisory Committee, Soviet Section. Rumor had it that she could trace her ancestry all the way back to Joseph Stalin. Yake looked up curiously.

"You have been—what is right word here? Set up? *Da.* Led by your noses down a primrose garden."

"Yes, of course, Ms. Poparov," Anne Larson, the British Representative, replied with a smile. "Considering your own political background, you would be the one most likely to spot such a situation—"

"This is not time for accusations and recriminations," Madja responded quietly. "This is time for thoughtful solutions."

"Absolutely." Larson's smile grew dangerous. "Let the record show that as soon as Ms. Poparov had read her accusations and recriminations into the record, she was ready to get back to work."

Madja's face reddened. "That is unfair attack. Very *nyekulturno.*"

"No attack is unfair—attacks are supposed to hurt. That's how the game is played."

Yake lowered his face to his notepad, to hide his own smile.

"Can we please keep to the subject, ladies—?" interrupted a tired voice. Yake looked up. It was the Ambassador.

Normally, the old man kept out of the roll-up-your-sleeves-and-get-down-and-dirty part of the discussions until a consensus began to develop. For him to request that the participants of a free-for-all try to stay on track demonstrated just how urgent he felt the situation really was.

Both Larson and Poparov nodded their instant acquiescence—then exchanged withering glares. Yake waited to see if the Ambassador was going to add anything else, but the Old Man lapsed back into silence.

"Sir?" That was Kasahara from Intelligence. "There may be some evidence to support Ms. Poparov's assertion that we've been set up—"

Poparov's glare turned into a triumphant smile.

"—but I think the truth is much more that we've set ourselves up. With encouragement, perhaps, but I don't think we should try to pass the blame entirely onto the Dhroo."

Madja's glare faded. Anne Larson's smile broadened.

And the cacophony began again.

"What I want to know," interrupted someone else, "is how we're going to explain to humanity that we've sold them into slavery?"

"—can't win a war against the slugs. We'll have to—"

"—really need to buy time. As much as we can—"

"—but if we shut down our information requests, we'll be admitting our bankruptcy. It'll be a clear declaration of our intent to default. We can't for a moment suggest that we're up against it or they might initiate a premature foreclosure. We don't know what they might do. Besides, if we keep downloading, we might discover something that—"

"—need to begin preparing the home front. Maybe there's a pretty face we can put on this situation; call it an Inter-Galactic Peace Corps, or something—"

"Another issue to consider—this whole thing is so out of character for the Dhrooughleem. They'd rather die than insult a guest. There must be something else going on—"

"And maybe there is *nothing* else going on. Maybe we misinterpreted. Maybe the message is a simple expression of concern, and an offer of help—"

"Very unlikely," said Kasahara. The certainty of his tone cut through the chatter like a knife. "The Dhrooughleem are polite. Not stupid. They have as many ulterior motives as any other species on this rock."

"Maybe they're trying to trigger a panic over here—" suggested someone else.

"Well, they've succeeded in doing that," Larson acknowledged, brushing her sandy-colored hair back off her forehead; she was already fading to gray at the temples.

"No," said Kasahara. He leaned forward earnestly. "Even that much aggression is very out of character for them. The Dhrooughleem do not get aggressive—they get polite. Very, very polite. Given the circumstances, the politest thing that they can do is make the first offer. I expect that we're going to be getting quite a few other offers of indenture very soon—especially if we're as close to the debt limit as the Dhrooughleem Liaison says. No, the Dhrooughleem aren't being eager here; that would be discourteous, and they are *never* discourteous. They're bending themselves backward to be polite. It just so happens that in this case, being polite means giving us the earliest possible opportunity to resolve our information debt."

"And then there's this possibility—" said Yake quietly, and all eyes turned abruptly to him. It was the first time he'd spoken since the uproar began. "I suspect that the Dhrooughleem are indentured themselves to another species; I don't know which one. And I don't even know why I suspect this, but it might be worth the effort to look for some confirming evidence. If they are working off a debt of their own, and if we do indenture ourselves to them, then we get to work off not only our own indenture, but theirs as well."

There was silence around the table.

Yake added, "I'm beginning to think that there are very many complex layers of indenture here, so that whoever we might indenture ourselves to is going to be making a very good price off our work—"

"You talk as if indenture is inevitable—" suggested the Ambassador quietly.

"I think it may very well be. Sorry sir, but my sense of the InterChange is that it's a pyramid scheme—and somebody has to be on the bottom."

"*Da*," said Madja Poparov. "This is exactly what my government has been afraid of for all hundred and sixty-seven years we have been participating—that we would be trapped by alien imperialists. Now we know what that trap is. Did no one ever think we were going to have to pay this bill someday?''

"Nobody took it seriously," retorted Larson, "because nobody ever thought the bill would come due. Or that anyone would ever come by to collect. By the way, did the Soviet Union ever repay its World War II debts to Britain and the United States?''

"That is *not* the issue." Poparov looked annoyed. "Who was entrusted with this responsibility? And why haven't they been properly tried?''

"Ahem? We're getting off track again," suggested Yake. Both women glared at him.

The Ambassador stepped into the moment of silence with a question. "You said something a moment ago, Yake, something about a . . . pyramid scheme?''

"Yes, sir. Everybody pays the guy upstairs, and the guy on the top floor ends up flush. The guys on the bottom, however, get stuck with the bill for everything. I think that the InterChange is set up to put the new guys—that's us—in the basement.''

The Ambassador turned the thought over in his mind. "That's a very interesting analogy, Yake," he said finally. "But it condemns the whole InterChange.''

"Sorry, sir. That's just the way it looks to me.''

"Okay, let's assume it for one minute. Is the situation we're in accidental or deliberate? Did we do it ourselves out of our own ignorance, or . . . do you also think that the Dhrooughleem deliberately entrapped us?''

Yake hesitated. He was looking down the barrel of a .45 caliber question. He had to choose his words carefully. "It would seem to me, sir, that if the Dhroo do have an indenture of their own, it would be very much to their advantage to put us to work paying it off for them. And even if they don't, it is still to their advantage to assume custodianship. Frankly, sir—" Yake found it hard to say this next part. "I feel particularly unhappy with the circumstance. It feels like—*to me*—a personal betrayal. I thought that the Dhroo representative and I had created a very friendly working relationship. Now I feel as if I've been used. *Raped*—pardon my English. Because of these feelings, it might be inappropriate for me to continue to represent our position to the Dhroo. In fact, if you want my resignation, sir—"

"Don't be silly, Yake. It's all right with me if you get angry. In fact, it'd be all right with me if you were pissed as hell! And then it'd be even more all right if you used that anger as fuel for your efforts at finding a way out of this mess."

"Thank you, sir."

"*De nada.*" The Ambassador turned back to Kasahara then. "All right, Nori. Let's go back to your point. You say that they're just being polite, nothing more—"

"No, sir—I didn't say that. Not at all. What I said was, the Dhrooughleem don't get aggressive. They get polite. And now, they've gotten very, very polite with us."

"Hm," said the Ambassador. "In other words, that politeness may just be the way that they *express* their aggression."

"Yes, sir. It's possible."

"I see. They don't put out the bear traps, but neither do they tell you to watch out for them when they take you for a walk in the woods, is that it?"

Kasahara nodded his head in agreement. His black hair shone like metal. He flashed his teeth in a grim smile of appreciation at the Ambassador's analogy.

"Good. Then, let's assume, for the moment, that this *is* a trap. It may be a dangerous assumption because it could blind us to other ways of dealing with the situation, but let's make the assumption anyway and see if we can find any evidence to support this assertion or disprove it."

Abruptly, Yake realized something. He sat up straight in his chair and stared across the table at the Ambassador. The Old Man wasn't crumbling under the strain at all. He'd been playing possum, ignoring all the tumult and turmoil, quietly waiting for the uproar to wear itself out.

Yake grinned in appreciation. You don't get to be Ambassador from Terra without some cunning. After all the accusations and recriminations had been made, and the conversation had finally gotten down to specifics, the Ambassador had resumed control of the meeting. Very clever. He didn't waste his energy on the wrong things.

"Yake," asked the Ambassador. "You seem to have a thought on your mind?"

"Uh, yes sir. I do. Um—we need to find out if this is the standard operating procedure of the InterChange or if the slugs have broken some rule or other. And we need to be very discreet about this line of inquiry, too."

"Yes. A very good suggestion." The Ambassador turned to the bulldozer-shaped woman. "Library, I'll want a full scan of the InterChange Charter documents." The Ambassador pulled his clipboard to him and switched it on. He glanced at it only briefly, then looked up across the table again.

"Those of you who are currently involved in other negotiations, we're going to want to review each and every one of those to see if there are any other hidden agendas that we don't know about. We may find that we've stepped in a whole minefield here."

The Ambassador paused to rub his nose thoughtfully between his long, bony fingers, then continued softly. "A key question is just how frankly we can discuss this situation with any of our contacts. I won't call them allies. But uh . . . let's see what we can find out about indenture contracts. What kind of terms are usually offered to a client, how long does a species have to pay, what are the penalties for default, that kind of thing. Oh, yes—" He turned to a sad-looking man three seats away. "Ted, I know this is an unpleasant possibility, but you might as well begin looking at ways to sell it to the home office, if we have to—"

A
NIGHT
TO
DISMEMBER

The dinner had been excellent and K!rikkl was feeling gaudy and sated. The young Ki! clacked its mandibles in loud appreciation and recited a verbose poem of praise for the culinary masterpieces of Hnaxx's. G!ligglix's flesh had *indeed* proven juicy and sweet—and, if that were not enough blessing for one evening, K!rikkl was already looking forward to the mating with Rrr later this evening. That, too, would be all the sweeter, since K!rikkl's discovery that Rrr was a favored child of the prestigious and powerful Trrrl^t nest.

K!rikkl felt very, very satisfied. So satisfied, in fact, that it had already decided that should tonight's mating prove successful, then the specially trained grub that had made the whole thing possible should receive the honor of hosting the larvae. It would not only be the politic thing to do, it would also be the safest.

Besides, it was always best to destroy the evidence.

And . . . should it ever prove necessary, K!rikkl could always begin training a new grub after the Fn^rr awakened in the spring. During the three days of restoration festivals, when the dream-refreshed Fn^rr reclaimed their pavilions from the Ki! caretakers, there were always opportunities for personal expansion—and a young Ki! without the resources and backing of a major nest to draw upon had to be constantly available to the beneficence of fate. Of course, should the mating with Rrr prove fruitful, that state of affairs was likely to change for the better, and quite rapidly, too. The Trrrl^t nest was rumored to have many fine plantations in need of proper care and guidance. This Ki! felt like just the one for the job.

Yes, K!rikkl was satisfied. It reached out and stroked one of Rrr's foreclaws affectionately. The younger Ki! seemed deliciously limber; an additional benefit—it would be an enjoyable mating as well as profitable. K!rikkl rasped its hind legs together in a quick rattle of anticipation. Rrr bowed its head in acquiescence.

"Don't be so impatient, K!rikkl—" Hnaxx said casually. "There is plenty of time for you and Rrr to retire to the mating pavilion, but there is only a short time left for us to pick the bones of sweet G!ligglix. Your playing of the game was beyond superb. Please remain a little longer and enlighten us with more of your delicious observations on Nestlings strategy."

K!rikkl withdrew its claw politely from Rrr's forelimb and said quietly, "Yes, of course, dear Hnaxx. How could I be less than generous in repaying your own beneficence? I am at your service. What is it you wish to know?" K!rikkl lowered its head in acquiescence.

"A simple thing, really." Hnaxx made a gesture that signified minimal importance, a squeezing motion with its foreclaws. "Tell me—how did you discover that a host-grub could be trained to help you cheat at Nestlings?"

"I beg your pardon?" K!rikkl swiveled its head in Hnaxx's direction. It actually *hadn't* understood the question—and then the meaning of the words did sink in, and K!rikkl was sorry it had responded at all.

"Ah," chirruped Hnaxx. "Perhaps you didn't notice the small black ornaments hanging from the rafters—"

K!rikkl jerked its triangular head up and around, blinking in confusion. There were several shining metal objects hung at intervals around the ceiling. K!rikkl had assumed that those were simply baubles, expensive off-world ornaments. The Fn^rr were fond of such. K!rikkl looked back to Hnaxx, keeping its face carefully impassive.

"But surely, you have heard of these devices, K!rikkl," said Hnaxx. "They are called cameras. They are the eyes and the ears of those who have lost their trust."

K!rikkl considered its responses carefully before responding. At last, it blinked slowly and rasped, "Perhaps *I* should be offended that you do not trust me—that you hang alien devices in a sacred pavilion."

Hnaxx declined the opportunity to apologize. "Perhaps *we* should be offended that you are not trustworthy. The devices were purchased from the same off-world slugs who negotiated our colonization here. They clearly show that your grub opened and examined the contents of every pouch on the table. But come—" Hnaxx dropped a blue silk cloth on the table and said, "—Let us not let the old rituals stand in the way of the success of our movements. The game was played and the conclusion has been celebrated. The claw of contention is not how you won, dear K!rikkl. Indeed, we can express only our admiration for your cleverness. We have been watching your career for some time and with much awe and wonderment; but we had not suspected such an ingenious device. Please tell us, how did you train it?"

"Train . . . it?" K!rikkl paused to consider its remaining options. They were all unpleasant. Of course, there was always the truth. . . .

"Come, come, K!rikkl—you are letting your fear do your thinking. Let me reassure you that you are in no danger at all here; you are among colleagues. You are in a position to do yourself, and many others as well, a great deal of good."

K!rikkl pounced upon the thought. That could be its single advantage here. The Ki! arched its head coyly sideways. "May I ask how?"

Hnaxx rasped its hind claws in annoyance. It looked up at the alien devices and then back to K!rikkl. It sighed. "This grows tiresome. Perhaps we need to take a walk in the moonlight to clear our heads. Will you join me?"

K!rikkl seized upon the idea eagerly. "It would be an honor, dear Hnaxx," and followed the older, larger Ki! toward the darkness beyond the pavilion.

They high-stepped in silence through the tufted loin-grass, across the barren meadow and down toward the gnarled wall-forest. Hnaxx deliberately steered K!rikkl away from the Fnˆrr groves. "Do not think me rude, but sometimes I find the scent of the Fnˆrr blossoms to be so sweet that it is almost overpowering. Sometimes I need to stand at a distance to admire them more appropriately."

"You need not apologize to me, great Hnaxx. I understand completely. The Fn⌢rr are such a grand race that I am occasionally inspired to—you must forgive me even for expressing such an indelicacy—but I do admit to an occasional twinge of . . . resentment.''

"Resentment?''

"Perhaps that is too strong a word; but I am young and impetuous. It is difficult to speak of indenture without chafing.''

."Yes, it is.'' Hnaxx did not speak again until they were safely within the broad bandwork of roots and traveling vines of the wall-forest. "I can only admire your caution, dear K!rikkl; that speaks well of your mind. It shall be of great service, if it is applied wisely.''

K!rikkl nodded its thanks, but said nothing.

Hnaxx continued quietly. "Let me explain something to you. Tonight's game was not simply a game of Nestlings. It was a carefully constructed pouch. We wanted to see who would grab it.''

"You are saying that the game was . . . contrived?''

Hnaxx clacked its mandibles in annoyance. "That would be an unforgivable rudeness to the guests. Even to suggest it is an offensive act.''

"I would abase myself publicly before committing such a terrible rudeness,'' K!rikkl responded quickly. "Nonetheless, what else am I to surmise from your assertion?''

"Ah,'' said Hnaxx. "Let me suggest this—that there was no way that you could have won any of tonight's cycles based on what was knowable to you. The only way to win this pouch was to know what was hidden in it and play accordingly. Whoever won this game tonight could only have done so by performing some maneuver not commonly accepted in the game of Nestlings. I shall be unconscionably direct—and please forgive my rudeness in being so, dear K!rikkl.''

K!rikkl waved away the apology. "We are colleagues.'' K!rikkl knew that was a presumption, but maybe a life-saving one.

"That you cheated,'' continued Hnaxx, "demonstrated to all of us that you are a Ki! well worthy of marrying into the

Trrrl^t nest. The cameras were hung not to determine *if* you cheated, only *how*. Had you not cheated, you would have been a tender feast, young Ki!.''

K!rikkl shuddered.

"So," Hnaxx added quietly, "you have no secrets except one—and now that you are about to become a member of the Trrrl^t nest, so must your knowledge also become a part of the common store. It is only appropriate."

K!rikkl acknowledged with a nod. "You are more clever than I suspected, noble Hnaxx. Had I realized—" K!rikkl rasped in annoyance and stopped in mid-phrase. There was really nothing to say.

K!rikkl held up a claw for error-apology, reformulated its thoughts, and began again. "My apologies for underestimating the cleverness of the Trrrl^t nest. I will endeavor to be worthy of the brilliance demonstrated here tonight."

They paused on a high, looping gnarl-branch and looked down at the jeweled pavilion and the vale beyond. The sprawling orchards were bathed in the soft pink glow of the moons. "The Fn^rr blossoms are fragrant tonight," said Hnaxx. "There will be many fine seedlings soon."

"And many more families. And many more pavilions." K!rikkl did not add the obvious. *And much more pressure on the Ki! to protect the young. The indenture will be exhausting*.

Hnaxx rasped its foreclaws in agreement. "What I am about to tell you has never happened. It is only hypothetical. So it means nothing. But even as a speculation, it is still a secret of the nest and must be guarded as carefully as an egg pouch. Do you understand?"

"I so acknowledge," said K!rikkl with ritual deliberation.

"Thank you." Hnaxx took K!rikkl by the forelimb and led the young Ki! back into the sheltering darkness of the wall-forest. "The Trrrl^t nest has been studying these grubs for some time. I myself have spent much time examining their dissected brains. We have often suspected that they might be capable of some higher logical behavior than we have ever seen demonstrated. Perhaps they could even be *trained* to eat or not to eat certain foodstuffs. Do you understand? It is something that we would like to experiment with. Your discoveries could be very valuable in ways I need not elucidate here. I'm sure you are smart enough to comprehend what I am saying.''

K!rikkl sighed. This was better than it had hoped. ''Yes, my lord.''

''Ahh, quite. So you can see why we are understandably curious. Where did you find out this knowledge? Who have you told? How have you applied it? Is this the only grub you have ever trained, or are there others in the hands of other Ki!? And what, if anything, have they discovered?''

''Let me be quick to reassure you. There are no others who share this knowledge, oh mighty Hnaxx. I myself was taught only by a traveling merchant who died soon after.''

''That is to your benefit, dear K!rikkl. Unfortunate for the merchant, but fortunate for you. It means that there is no one else whose knowledge is as valuable as yours. This has great bearing on a question that the Trrrl̂t nest has been considering for some time: what value might these grubs have beyond their obvious uses as food or hosts for our larvae? I need not tell you how much *our* nest might benefit if we had the answers to such questions.''

K!rikkl nodded its agreement, at the same time trying to hide its glee. The opportunities here could be extraordinary! And dangerous as well! What a very *interesting* dilemma!

Hnaxx paused to rasp its foreclaws in anticipation. ''That is why you were invited to play in the game this evening. Your success at the game of Nestlings has improved remarkably since you have begun traveling with a host-grub. We were most curious about this fact, and I tell you truly, we had not expected such an astonishing demonstration. We find it most interesting to see that your grub is capable of such astonishing behavior. It suggests possibilities to us that we had not previously dreamed of. Now do you see why we need to know how this grub was trained?''

K!rikkl's mind was racing with thoughts of unlimited wealth and unnumbered mates. Perhaps even a nest of its own! Was it truly possible to dream this big? K!rikkl bent its forelimbs and lowered its head in acquiescence. "I shall be at the service of your nest, my lord. My flesh is yours."

"Thank you, K!rikkl," said Hnaxx. "Your service is accepted and welcomed into this nest. And in return, the nest stands ready to serve you."

THE
COLD
EARTH

Into the southern hemisphere of a gentle world comes a night when the blossoms rustle with tomorrow's wind.

The hot breath of unborn days catches the leaves of many orchards, many groves, and all the stands arise to wakefulness in hours, all the stands, all whispering with the troubled murmurings a dream-time less than sweet.

The blossom-scents of many Fn^rr turn yellow-brown with dreadfulness and uncertainty.

My roots have grown so cold. . . .

The hideous dreams, they come again!

The sense is clear. The scent is fear.

My roots are cold!

There is ash upon the soil.

We wither and we die.

There are eaters in the dreams. Many eaters creeping. They eat the seeds. They eat the young. They scoop and eat the brains of those who dream.

My roots are cold.

The eaters come, the eaters breed, they run wild in the groves! They eat us as we dream!

All cry for seedlings yet unsown!

Where are the Ki!? Where are the Ki!?

Where is the promise of the garden-keepers?

Why are the Ki! not in the dreams? Is the rasp of silver claws so much like the sound of teeth?!

Fear for the Ki!, the ones who walk the night. They swarm and spread betrayal of the crop.

My roots are cold.

Fear for the Ki! No more to swarm! No more to swarm!

They are lost in dreamless dreams! They do not heed our cries!

The dreams, the foul dreams!

39

Who brings such madness to the roots? Who fouls the dreams?

Who?

The wet ones slither through the dreams.

The wet ones lie in slime! They promised us a world! Ai-eee. It is a world of death!

My roots are very cold.

The dreams are filled with teeth and terror!

The eaters still infest the groves, they overrun the groves. The orchards swarm with menace. The soil blackens with manure. The children die within their hands!! The wind does roar and rip the leaves!

Why do these dreams infest? What portends? What horrors sweep upon us from the night beyond the dawn? Why are the dreadful eaters following on the trail of the slugs?

So cold. So very cold.

Abandon hope. Abandon fear. The edge of horror soon cuts here!

The slugs are beasts from coldest hell, from hottest hell, from driest hell, from wettest hell. They speak in lies; they lie in offal. The awful truth of slugs is that slugs can't tell the truth!

The wet ones creep through all the dreams. They speak too sweetly; they leave behind a sugary death. They give our children no safe place to sink their roots.

We have been sliced.

Betrayed.

Destroyed.

My roots are cold.

The eaters come through coldest night. Can you hear the teeth?

The dreams are screams of children, seedlings dreaming screaming! They are being eaten in their birth-dreams!!

The stalks of many will soon be rotting in the dream-groves!

The death comes quickly, spreading like a brown and wilting scour.

Aieee!! I mourn! I mourn!

Our world will be lost, our blossoms fall upon a barren land!

We can no longer trust the hosting slugs! They kill us with their kindness!

There is no hope! No hope! No home!

So very very cold.

Abandon home, all ye who have grown here!

No place to sink our roots!

No place at all!

We roam through airless voids!

Again to dream of other worlds, other voices? Can we dream of other land?

Dream a voice. Dream a voice. A sound of light.

There is no voice. Only the grunting sounds of eaters.

Too bold. Too bold. There are no roots in space.

So very, very bold.

Neither is there soil in which to nurture a tomorrow.

Can we no longer sense new scents upon the solar wind? Have our branches grown so stiff?

There are no voices.

And even so, is there not a hint of wonder? Can such things be possible?

There is always room for wonder.

Can there be a voice of light within the dreams? A ray of sun in which to grow?

The dreams have all been fouled.

Can we afford to send our seedlings into space to seek these other voices?

Can the grove afford to risk the danger?

And even as the dream comes down, can we not afford to take the chance?

That is the root of the question.

The root. The solid root.

Can we not afford to take the chance?

We must . . . negotiate.

We must.

My roots are cold.

AN
OFFER
OF
EMPLOYMENT

The Ambassador cleared his throat for attention and the room fell abruptly silent. Yake was suddenly conscious of just how old the Old Man really looked. Maybe it wasn't *all* performance. He felt embarrassed at the thought, as if he'd penetrated some private part of the Old Man's self.

But then the Ambassador spoke, and his voice was as strong and commanding as ever—and all thoughts of the man's fragility fell completely out of Yake's consciousness.

"All right," the Ambassador was saying. "We've begun receiving some responses to our, ah . . . inquiries about the possibilities of humanity's service to the InterChange. I won't comment on the ones that I've seen. I think that the, ah . . . acceptability of these will be self-evident. Nori?"

Kasahara opened the folder in front of him and began reading slowly. "Yes, sir." Kasahara looked around the table. His usual good-natured smile was missing as he turned to the first of the papers in his folder. "I'll read these in the order received.

"The Nixies of Nn have offered a six percent premium for human service as larval incubators. We have to guarantee a minimum of five hundred thousand nonrefundable individuals per mating cycle. Seven point one percent if we maintain a breeding station onsite. No colonial rights are implied. Severe penalties for failure to meet quota. Although the Nixies say they're planning to colonize several new worlds, Intelligence suspects that they are actually increasing their breeding in preparation for a war to be held not less than seven years from now, probably thirteen."

Kasahara did not wait for any reactions to that. He turned the page and immediately began reading the next. "The Dragons are willing to purchase—that's a flat-out purchase; we can apply the credits any way we choose—one to three

45

million nonrefundable individuals per year. Two credits per body, plus fifteen percent allowance for shipping. Live bodies only. This is a no-explanations, take-it-or-leave-it deal. The offer is a standing one, always open, but the terms are nonnegotiable. The Dragons guarantee nothing but immediate payment.''

"Analysis?" asked the Ambassador.

Kasahara held up a single flimsy. "Intelligence reports that the Dragons prefer to eat their prey live.''

Someone at the far end of the table gasped. Yake resisted the temptation to look around; he kept his face impassive. He had a hunch it was going to get worse. Much worse.

The Ambassador ignored the exclamation. "Go on, Nori.''

"Um, yes—" Kasahara turned to the next document. "Um, there's an inquiry here from a race of . . . I guess you could call them intelligent plants. Apparently, they're having some trouble with vermin. They're curious about our abilities as . . . the only word that translates is—'' Kasahara scratched his ear embarrassedly, ''—gardener.''

"Mm hm.'' The Ambassador nodded. "Let's get back to them on that one. Ask them for more details on what they need. Go on.''

"The J(kk)l and the J(rr)l are both willing to purchase frozen or dead individuals. They won't pay as much as the Dragons, only one credit per body, but they are willing to assume the full cost of shipping. They have their own fleet. They're willing to pick up on-site. All we have to do is provide them with the coordinates of our home system.''

"I don't like the sound of that—'' someone said.

"Hush,'' said the Ambassador. "We're not discussing acceptability yet.'' He nodded to Kasahara again.

"Um—we also have six similar offers from—'' Kasahara started leafing quickly through his papers.

"Never mind,'' interrupted the Ambassador. "We'll get to them when we get to them. Keep going.''

"Yes, sir.'' Kasahara swallowed hard and turned to the next page.

"We have four more inquiries similar to the Nixies'.

These are all routine; we haven't met any of their liaison people. Apparently larval incubators are in great demand all over the InterChange—or it's going to be quite a war. The Sslyb, the Whroolph, the Ki!—I don't know if I pronounced any of those right—and the Mnxorn, have all tendered inquiries of availability, based on proven species compatibility—compatibility to be determined through hands-on testing; we assume the costs of the testing and providing suitable specimens. No bids from any of them until biocompatibility is established to a 66 percent minimum."

Kasahara looked troubled for a moment, then added, "Analysis Section raises a serious question here, sir."

"What is it?"

"Well . . . have the Nixies established biological compatibility already? If so, *how?* None of the other species have claimed it—and none of the others have offered bids, either." Kasahara was having a little difficulty reading the next part. "Analysis suggests that a deeper investigation may be mandated here. Perhaps the Nixies have already been experimenting with—"

"Nori—" The Ambassador interrupted gently. "If they have, there's nothing we can do about it. Not yet, anyway. Just keep reading."

"Yes, sir." Kasahara turned to the next page. "The slugs—sorry, sir, I mean, the Dhrooughleem—"

"Slugs is acceptable to me," said the Ambassador. "What are the slugs offering?"

"Well, they've very reluctantly withdrawn their previous offer. They have expressed great shame and embarrassment, but apparently our going public is seen as a great loss of trust in their ability to manage our indenture benevolently."

"Yes, yes." The Old Man made a gesture of annoyed impatience. "So what are the slugs offering now?"

"Three credits. Per body."

"For what service?"

"I'm not certain. It doesn't seem to translate well. It's— it's guaranteed to be a dry-land service. The individuals are guaranteed refundable, but—the reprogramming is not guaranteeable."

"Reprogramming?"

"Apparently, there will be some psychological adjustments needed for this particular service; upon completion of service, full restoration of previous mental condition may not be possible. Sir, I—I'm having a great deal of trouble with this—"

"So are we all, Nori. Please go on."

"Well, the slugs' offer almost looks like a pretty good one, until you get into the details. They're asking only for female individuals—"

"Did they say for what purpose?"

"No, sir. Do you want me to ask?"

"Uhh . . . I'd rather you didn't. I don't think I'd like the answer. Never mind, go on."

"Uh—yes, sir." Kasahara turned the page gratefully. "Independently, we've determined that we can probably place a half-million individuals per year in various tourist facilities. That's more a courtesy than a source of income, but it does credit us with triple bonuses against the interest on our debt."

"Tourist facilities?" interrupted Madja.

"Zoos," said Kasahara. "On some planets, there's considerable curiosity about who else lives in the galaxy. There are over a hundred thousand major zoos served by the InterChange. Fortunately, we're listed as a herding species, so they'd have to take a minimal size representation—no less than fifty individuals per facility, no more than six million."

"Six million?"

"That's for the colony creatures—ants, bees, termites, bacteriological colonies and the like. I think we'd be limited to several hundred individuals per facility; but even so, that would give us at least one form of acceptable service, and the payments on our interest would be large enough to justify the effort. Unfortunately, the payments are only against the interest; none of it can be credited against the principal—so even though the zoo option can help control the rate of growth of our debt, it can't provide us with any kind of a permanent solution."

"Good," said the Ambassador. "Anything else?"

"Um. Yes." Kasahara was already looking ahead to the next offer. He glanced up with a paler-than-usual expression. "Uh—we have an offer from a consortium of six neo-reptilian species. They're willing to accept our entire indenture as it currently stands, plus a yearly stipend for future information acquisitions."

"Well, that sounds more like it!" remarked one of the younger assistants. He was ignored by almost everyone at the table.

"Right," said the Ambassador. "What do they want to buy?"

"Um . . . they want the right to begin biological experimentation on the human species—with an eye toward eventually mutating us into something useful. For one thing, they don't think we have enough sexes; that's why we breed so fast. However, they do guarantee no resale of individuals for either food or larval incubators—"

"Hm, I wonder if we could do that one with volunteers?" suggested Anne Larson.

Kasahara looked across the table at her. "They require a minimum of one hundred thousand nonrefundable units per month for experimentation, plus total autonomy over the species' colonization and growth—uh, that includes the homeworld."

"That answers that," said Larson.

The Ambassador's expression was unreadable. He merely offered, "I think we might have some difficulty presenting that option to the home office. Please go on, Nori."

"Yes, sir. We also have two inquiries from bacteriological colonies. They're asking if we would consent to biological compatibility testing. If compatibility is possible, they would like to open negotiations for a symbiotic relationship. Um—these species don't live on worlds, they live inside other species. Two viral species have also requested testing, I think. I'm not sure this was translated correctly. We'd have to guarantee freedom from antibiotic and white-cell contamination. They guarantee no protection for the hosts; mostly they seem to be interested in breeding sites. Maybe they're preparing for a war, too? Along the same lines, several

parasitical races have indicated their willingness to um
. . . test for biological compatibility."

"Hmf," said the Ambassador noncommittally. "Do we
have any offers from Smallpox, Leprosy or Psoriasis?"

"Just a moment," said Kasahara, thumbing quickly
through the stack of papers in front of him. "I'll look—"

"Nori," the Old Man reached over and put a hand on
Kasahara's arm. "That was a joke."

"A joke?" Kasahara blinked. "Oh. A joke."

"It's all right, Nori. You can look them up later. Please
go on. Do you have any others to present?"

"Just two more, sir—the Rhwrhm have inquired if our
planet is available for colonization; payment proportional to
the number of colonists allowed to settle. Uh, the Rhwrhm
are carnivores, sir. Very *large* carnivores. They eat
Dragons."

"Yes, I see. And the other offer?"

"That's from the Rh/attes. They're suggesting something
very unusual—unusual for the InterChange, that is. They
don't need any service that we can provide—nothing important, that is, although they're willing to buy a couple of
million tons of corn per year; but that's mostly a courtesy—
a gesture of friendship from one mammalian species to
another. What they're suggesting instead is that we assume
their indenture."

"I beg your pardon?" The Old Man took off his glasses
and began to clean them with his handkerchief. "I don't
think I heard you right." He returned his spectacles to his
face and peered owlishly through them at the younger man.
His eyes seemed very large and bright. "There. That's
better. Now, try that on me again."

"They want us to assume a piece of their indenture,"
repeated Kasahara.

"That's what I thought you said." The Ambassador
looked surprised. He glanced down the table to Miller, the
head of Analysis Section. "Has your section had a chance
to consider the implications of that?"

Miller shook her head. "It doesn't make sense to us.
We're in much bigger trouble than the Rh/attes. We can't

pay our own bills, let alone theirs. What do they gain here? Assuming we find a way to avoid defaulting, the only guarantee we can give them is that we're not going to sell them to anyone for food, incubation, or sex; nor will we sell them for biological experimentation without their consent. I don't see that that's strong enough to justify putting their fate in our hands. They can guarantee that by themselves right now. We have no real use for them; apparently no one else does, either. So, the alternative is that there's some advantage for them to be indentured to a species that defaults."

"I'll bet a nickel I know what it is," put in Larson.

The Ambassador looked down the table at her. "Yes, Anne?"

"It's really very simple—if we assume their indenture, we assume the total burden of their debt. When we default, we have to work off their debt as well as ours—and they go free. It's an easy way for them to wipe out their debt all at once."

"Interesting," said the Ambassador. "And quite clever in its own way. Hm. Let me consider the other side of that question for a moment. Is there any advantage in it for us? Could we—excuse me for asking this—structure the deal so that we could . . . ah, create some advantage here?"

"You mean, could we sell them as food, fuel, slaves, sex or guinea pigs?" Larson shook her head. "The Rh/attes are considered almost as undesirable as we are by the reptilian and insectoid species. Their debt isn't as large because they never downloaded as heavily as we did. On the other hand, neither have they ever come up with a service that the InterChange considers valuable; so they might be in just as tenuous a situation as we are. But they've been around for nearly five hundred years, so the real question is *why* hasn't the InterChange foreclosed on them? What service do the Rh/attes provide that justifies their current status?"

"You have some idea?" the Old Man asked.

Larson shrugged. "I'm not sure that this is a useful avenue of exploration, but if we knew how they had lasted five hundred years, it might shed some light on the details of their offer to us." She sighed tiredly. "I'm sorry, sir, but knowing that the Rh/attes are mammalian, I'd distrust them more than all the others put together. I know how nasty and greedy mammals can be.''

"Unfortunately, I'm inclined to agree with you," the Ambassador said. He looked to Kasahara. "Is that it?"

"I'm afraid so, sir."

"All right—" The Old Man did not look beaten. "Let's do it this way. We'll break the offers down into four categories—" He began to tick them off on his fingers. "Totally Unacceptable, Not Bloody Likely, Need More Information, and Let's Talk. We'll break into committees; each committee will evaluate three proposals and then validate the work of two other committees—"

A
QUIET
OBJECTION

"Excuse me, sir!"

"Eh?" The Ambassador looked down the table. "Is there an objection?"

"Yes sir, there is." Madja Poparov stood up. "I object to this whole proceeding. We are talking about the future of the human species."

"Yes, Ms. Poparov, we are. What is your point?"

"That *is* my point. Are we qualified to do this job—to make these decisions?"

The Ambassador nodded politely while he considered her question. At last he looked across the table at her and responded in a quiet tone of voice.

"Whether we're qualified or not is irrelevant. The responsibility is still ours. I grant you that none of us here sought out or even desired this responsibility—most of us thought we were merely signing on for diplomatic research—but the circumstances have changed dramatically in the past few days. So have our jobs. Now, we have only *one* decision to make. Are we going to accept the responsibility that's been thrust upon us, or shirk it? If we choose not to accept the responsibility, we must still accept the consequences of that choice."

"I do not dispute that," said Madja. "Idiot I am not. The Union of Soviet Socialist Republics does not send fools to the front. I know that the choice must be made here, if for no other reason than there simply is not *time* to send back home for a decision. The issue I am raising, Mr. Ambassador, is this one: how can we justify this discussion at all? How can we give any seriousness to these proposals? They are *all* unacceptable because of the context that acceptance of any of them would create."

She paused, as if waiting for applause.

There was none.

Madja Poparov brushed her hair back off her forehead and continued. "The trouble with you capitalists is that you are too damned pragmatic. We are sitting here and calmly discussing a set of possibilities that reduce human beings to the status of draft animals—or worse!

"We are talking about selling our brothers and sisters—*our comrades in the human adventure!*—into slavery as food or guinea pigs or hosts for parasitical life forms! And zoo animals, no less!

"The best of these offers that Mr. Kasahara has read to us is the one that at least gives us the dignity of a common farm laborer—and even that one is unacceptable because it says that human beings have not the wit to do anything more than follow someone else's instructions. I say that we cannot consider seriously any course of action that would establish that human beings are anything less than a noble species. This is the real issue. We must let them know that we deserve nothing less than the highest respect! Or—" Madja looked grim and unhappy, "—we shall be condemning ourselves and our children to a future of slavery and despair for untold generations to come."

This time there was applause.

But only from Yake.

He clapped loudly in the silence—and his applause was clearly intended as a sarcastic response to the melodramatic style of Madja's presentation.

Everybody else just looked uncomfortable.

Madja glared down the table at Yake. "You think this is funny, Mr. Yake Singh Browne?"

"The situation, no. The speech, maybe."

"You do not like what I said?"

Yake shrugged. "I question whether such speeches make much of a difference in the long run."

"The difference is whether we live as a free people or as slaves! Is that not difference enough?"

Yake shrugged again. "I won't argue the question. I do find it . . . amusing that the distinction should be coming from you, Ms. Poparov. That is, from a representative of the Soviet Union.''

Madja frowned at Yake.

Madja Poparov's frown was a formidable expression.

Madja Poparov's frown had been known to wither a rose bush at thirty meters.

She now turned the full force of it on Yake Singh Browne, a smug, self-satisfied, hot-blooded young parasite of the imperialistic ruling class of the degenerate societies of the western hemisphere—

Yake returned her stare, nonplussed.

The Old Man cleared his throat then; he allowed himself a drink of water, then cleared his throat again. He looked down the table at the two of them. ''Yake—did you want to address the issue here? Ms. Poparov raised the issue of contextual repositioning inherent in the offers . . . ?''

Yake regretted having to tear his eyes away from Madja. Actually, she had very nice eyes. But—reluctantly, he turned to the head of the table and said, ''Well, yes sir, I did—''

Everyone at the table turned to face him. Yake could understand their curiosity. He, too, wondered what he was about to say. ''It seems to me that Madja here—pardon, I mean, Ms. Poparov—has raised a critical point. Um. One that is worthy of considerable . . . uh, consideration.'' Yake realized he was about to start sounding stupid. He caught himself and began again, ''What I mean is—I think Madja is right.''

The Ambassador did not look pleased with that response. Clearly, he had been hoping for a different sort of rebuttal.

Yake continued quickly. ''If I were going to take the usual *pragmatic* view of the situation, I might say that we should choose the least unacceptable of these possibilities and make the best of a terrible situation. I could remind Ms. Poparov that we are a mammalian species, and that, as it has turned out in the grand scheme of things, mammalian intelligence is not a common occurrence, but only the occasional fluke of evolution that occurs when some disaster interrupts the natural trend to intelligence in reptilian and insect species. On our own world, a comet smacked into the planet 65 million years ago and the resulting "nuclear winter" killed off the dinosaurs. There's a lot of evidence to suggest that Hadrosaurs were just reaching the threshold of sentience. Who knows what they could have become? But primitive mammalian ancestors, like the Therapsids, evolved to fill the dinosaurs' ecological niches too quickly, and the dinosaurs never got the chance to reestablish themselves. To most of the species in the InterChange, we're the descendants of ecological interlopers—uh, we're Darwinian carpetbaggers.

"The membership of this InterChange is proof enough of that: two thousand and seventeen species, and only twelve of them are identifiably mammalian in nature—the rest are reptilian or insectoid, or otherwise unclassifiable.

"We may not like it," Yake said, "but the evolutionary patterns have been documented and confirmed by our own computers. As life climbs toward intelligence, the reptilian and insect species have the advantage—and on most of the worlds, that's who gets there first. The mammals never get a chance; we stay in our trees and our burrows while the thunder lizards conquer the sky. We are tree shrews, we are rats, we are spider-monkeys with delusions of grandeur." He looked to Madja Poparov regretfully. "It's difficult for me to listen seriously to talk about 'our comrades in the human adventure' when all of the evidence suggests that, at best, we are little more than accidents of evolution."

Madja Poparov sniffed. She looked like she wanted to reply, but Yake cut her off with a raised finger—

"If talking snakes and slugs and spiders are shocking and offensive to us, then consider what we must look like to them. We are egg-suckers and parasites and disease-spreaders, standing up on our hind legs and demanding a place at *their* banquet table; and they—despite their own charter—are horrified by us. They are as horrified as we would be if spirochetes and crab lice demanded representation at the United Council.

"The politest comparison I could make—" and here Yake spread his own brown hands before him, "—and I apologize for saying it, but it is still true—is that mammals, human beings in particular, are the 'outcasts' of the galaxy." He bowed to the woman on his east and added with elaborate politeness, "Or perhaps, if Ms. Poparov did not understand that, I could say that we are the Ukrainians here in this cosmic Politburo—only it's even worse than that analogy suggests. There is no *chance* of respect for us here—and very likely, not even for what we can bring to the membership of this body, because this body is not prepared to see us or deal with us as equals.

"*That* is what I would say if I were going to be *pragmatic*."

Yake hesitated for effect; he looked around the room, meeting all of their eyes deliberately—even the Ambassador's. He held up one forefinger to note that he had one more point to make, the most significant point of all. "*But*, if I were going to be *truly* pragmatic, I would look again at these choices before us and I would ask myself what problems will we be creating for ourselves if we accept *any* of these circumstances? What would be the consequences?

"The first thought that occurred to me was that we would be letting others determine the future of our species, not ourselves. It would be very difficult for human beings to maintain our sense of direction, our sense of responsibility under such disabling circumstances—and for that reason, I was considering voicing my own objections. I say 'considering' because my arguments were based on the intangible considerations of how we might 'feel' about these options; and, I admit it, I was thinking that our feelings in the matter might be the kind of illogical factor that throws the whole equation off. While I was sitting here pondering that dilemma, Madja spoke up and I saw that she had gone straight to the beating heart of the matter."

Yake looked to Madja now. "It really doesn't matter what decision we make here. If we accept *any* of these options, we will be saying to the rest of the membership of the InterChange that we are not worthy of respect, because we, too, see ourselves as nothing better than food or guinea pigs or zoo animals." Yake looked around the table. "I never thought I would say this, but I think Madja is right. All of these options are unacceptable, because in the long run they will damage us much more than they can possibly help us in the short term.''

Yake sat down again.

Madja Poparov looked surprised.

Madja Poparov looked *very* surprised.

Yake was very pleased with himself.

The Old Man himself was wearing a thoughtful expression. He did not look happy, but neither did he look angry. Merely . . . thoughtful.

At last he cleared his throat and said, "Thank you, Yake. You've raised several points that I think all of us need to keep in mind. Yes. The situation is a complex one. Um. What you and Ms. Poparov have pointed out is quite true. From a philosophical point of view, the solutions before us are indeed very difficult ones. Unfortunately, they're the only solutions available to us. Hm. Let me suggest something here. Suppose you and Madja Poparov and—how about Anne Larson, too? And Nori as well—constitute yourselves as an *ad hoc* committee to explore what, if any, acceptable alternatives may be available to us, while the regular staff continues to evaluate the options we've discussed today. Yes, I think that will work. All right. Any comments?''

There were none.

Yake and Madja exchanged unhappy glances, but neither voiced an objection. Anne Larson looked stricken. Even Nori Kasahara looked unhappier than usual.

The Ambassador added then, "I've ordered the kitchen to stay open all night. Full meal service until two A.M., then sandwiches and coffee until breakfast. The staff secretaries are already letting your wives and husbands, girlfriends and boyfriends and others, know that you will be working late. We will reconvene at ten tomorrow. Any questions? None? Good. Thank you all.''

BEST
OF
THE
BREED

As the great red sun rose in the sky, it turned the day into a bright pink bath of light. All across the valleys, the Fn^rr were turning their broad leaves to its warming rays. Soon, they would be walking again.

It was not a pleasant thought.

K!rikkl realized that too many of the Fn^rr had survived the dream-time. Despite the ever-increasing ravages of the brain-eating vermin, most of the orchards on the southern continent had still come through the winter relatively unscathed by the parasites—more than half of the new crop of Fn^rr had survived. This meant much more pressure on the Ki! very soon. There would be many more pavilions built, and that meant far fewer swarming grounds. Already, many Ki! lived their entire lives without ever having the opportunity to swarm.

It could be a bad time for the Ki! on this world, K!rikkl thought; it would be well to be allied with the Trrrl^t nest.

"You were considering something?" Hnaxx asked, coming up to join K!rikkl on the high branch.

"Ahh, just some idle musings about the possibilities for the future."

"Yes, the view from here is quite lovely." Hnaxx looked out over the valley. "The Fn^rr are such beautiful beings. It is too bad that they are ravaged so by these vermin. It is quite to our benefit—and theirs—that we can make such good use of the terrible grubs."

"Quite," agreed K!rikkl. "But it is too bad that they were even on this world in the first place."

"Agreement on that as well," nodded Hnaxx. "Let me ask you something. Don't you find it odd that creatures as ugly and distasteful as these vermin can occupy so much of our attention?"

63

"Odd, no. Unfortunate, yes. It is a well-known fact that intelligent beings tend to focus too much on their own diseases and dysfunctions. It is one of the primary curses of sentience."

"Ahh, you are a wit as well," rattled Hnaxx gaily. "That is a skill that will be much appreciated at the table." The older Ki! put a claw on K!rikkl's forelimb. "But, let me be impatient now—as long as we are discussing such an unfortunate subject, let us carry it to its conclusion and be done with it once and for all. You were going to instruct me on the training of the grubs."

"A pitiful discussion, really. There is not that much to tell."

"I am interested in it nonetheless."

"The creatures are disappointingly simple," said K!rikkl. "Really, they are not much good for anything. They taste too gamey to be good food, and they are inefficient larval incubators; it takes too long for one to grow large enough to hold more than a few eggs. They die too easily during implantation and give off fearful stenches when they decompose."

"Yes, that is well known to all of us, dear K!rikkl," chided Hnaxx. "But you promised to tell us things we did not know."

"Truly, my lord. I just wanted to point out what a useless species these grubs may be, even for the most common purposes we use them for. Despite their prevalence on this world, they are really quite an affront to nature as we know it. The skin is too thin, it punctures too easily; the flesh is too warm, and too soft for good eating, although it is tasty; they are not much more than warm bags of salt and ichor." K!rikkl lowered its voice and added, "Indeed, there is even a theory among some breeders that a Ki! hatched in the body of one of these grubs has been insufficiently nourished during its larval stage and may perhaps be mentally deficient."

"I was hatched in one of these grubs," remarked Hnaxx dryly.

"Ah, well . . . then that theory is clearly disproven. I am

truly glad to know that. I will stop the spread of this pernicious rumor wherever I hear it.''

"It is of no importance," replied Hnaxx. "It is well known that the Trrrl⁀t nest hatches all of its larvae in specially selected grubs. That should be proof enough of the falsity of such malicious gossip.''

K!rikkl hesitated as it considered the portent of Hnaxx's words. Had it stepped in something sticky here? Probably. Was the situation irreversibly damaged? Possibly. But perhaps not. K!rikkl hoped not. Indeed, K!rikkl could only proceed as if it had not committed an irretrievable offense. It polished its foreclaws politely and continued, "The point is, my lord, that despite all of the many purposes to which we put these animals, these creatures are overrated in their usefulness.''

Hnaxx nodded its agreement. "This is well known to many Ki!. The grubs are vermin. Oh, they are occasionally useful as pack animals, and you can see many of them on the road pulling lorries. I must admit that they are at least wonderful for the disposal of garbage, and the youngsters delight in riding them for sport; they are also quite suited for heavy labor and even for the simplest of routine chores—but aside from these few minimal purposes, it would be a blessing for all of us if they were to be exterminated completely. There are far more useful creatures available to us for all of these tasks, and certainly the Fn⁀rr would have no objection to the extinction of a life form that has been known to prey on the Dreamers of Winter.''

"Certainly not.''

"Well, there you have it," said Hnaxx. "That is why it was so clever of you to train one. They are so useless that no one would suspect.''

K!rikkl nodded in modest acceptance of the compliment. "I did nothing that could not have been done by any careful and persevering Ki!. I must confess, though, that these creatures can be quite tiresome. Training one is no task for a Ki! with an impatient disposition.''

"I can well imagine, dear K!rikkl—but please elucidate.''

K!rikkl barked a command to its grub; it came scuttling

across the floor and sat up before him. "A simple command, do you see? I make a specific sound and it performs a simple action. It looks too easy, but I tell you that it truly takes a great deal of time and patience to train one, and one cannot assume that the training will take. Beyond a certain size, the males are too hard to control and the females think of nothing but rutting. The creatures have great hormonal difficulties. It is amazing to me that they survive at all. Do you know that the female can only bear one young at a time? It crawls out of the belly completely helpless and must be cared for completely while it grows toward usefulness. During much of this time, the female is useless for further breeding. I truly do not understand why these creatures are not already extinct."

"Nor do I," said Hnaxx blandly. "But please, K!rikkl, tell me how you trained it."

"Of course, my lord. In principle, it is quite easy. A simple system of reward and punishment. I tie a rope to its neck. I rattle 'Come,' and pull the rope until it comes. Then I give it a tender root to chew. Soon it learns that if it wants a tender root, it should come when I say 'Come,' After that, the rest is details."

"It is that simple?" Hnaxx seemed astonished.

"Truly. All of the training is based on the same principle. If I hold up the game marker for a Knrkt and make it touch its toes, very soon it learns to touch its toes whenever it sees a Knrkt marker. Later, I train it to wait until I rattle my mandibles in annoyance. Then it touches its toes if it has seen a Knrkt marker only on my command. The rest of you think I am only grumbling in disgust—the grub tells me what it has seen and you think it is a distasteful creature. Poor G!ligglix never had a chance."

"Aiee—what an ingenious ploy, dear K!rikkl. I am delighted that you were so diplomatic in your play."

"It is bad manners to dine on the host," K!rikkl acknowledged.

"Your manners, dear K!rikkl, are as impeccable as your deceitfulness."

"Thank you, my lord."

"But I cannot get over how . . . simple it all seems."

"Simple indeed, Lord Hnaxx. But it does require patience—that is why there are not many grubs this well trained."

"That is lucky for us—or we might have to change the rules of the game. As it is, I foresee great possibilities inherent in this knowledge."

"Indeed?"

"Indeed."

THE
GANG
OF
FOUR

Madja Poparov could swear in six different languages.

At least that was how many Yake could identify before he lost count. There were several he couldn't identify. He simply listened in rapt admiration for several minutes before he attempted to interrupt.

"Excuse me," he said politely, "—I may be mistaken, but I think you repeated yourself there."

"I did not!"

"I think so, yes. The derogatory comparison between the breeding habits of pigs and capitalists; I think that parallels the statement you made about the copulatory practices of politicians and goats—"

Madja frowned as she attempted to recall what she had said several minutes earlier. "Is possible," she admitted. "I was being very enthusiastic."

Yake grinned. "Would you care to boil that communication down to its essential points?"

"Hmp. Is simple. *Ad hoc* committee is not a committee at all, Mr. Yake Singh Browne. The 'Old Man,' as you so lovingly refer to him, is acting like the consummate politician he is. You and I, we are troublemakers—I more than you. I raise unpleasant point in meeting. You make mistake of agreeing with me—"

"You were right—"

"Is still mistake. You agree, no? No matter. Ambassador does not want disagreement, but must demonstrate—in case there is trial later—that all points of view were fairly heard. He listens to you and me, then makes us special committee. Larson and Kasahara are here to give committee credibility, no?"

"No—" said Larson.

Poparov ignored her. "If just you and me, Yake, then it

71

looks like he is removing all his bad eggs from the same basket. But by putting other person here too, he invests committee with air of credibility. Very smart. If you and I come up with something, we get to be heroes; if we don't come up with something, we are—what? What is expression for empty-handed idealist?''

"Empty-handed idealist.''

"Yes. You and I, we have been put where we cannot cause any trouble. I am sorry I take you down with me. You are good manager. Not a good leader, but a good manager. Is two different things. I am good leader.''

"And modest, too.''

"Yes. Thank you for noticing.''

Yake blinked. Was that a serious response—or had she topped his own gibe? Sometimes with Madja Poparov it was hard to tell. He rubbed his hand through his bristly hair and scratched his head in puzzlement.

"You know,'' Kasahara interrupted, "you guys are both missing something. There might be another possibility here, too.''

"What?'' Anne Larson looked up for the first time.

"Maybe, just *maybe,* the Ambassador thinks we're smart enough to come up with something that nobody else can; a solution that isn't so damned *insulting.*''

"Is good point, Kasahara. I owe you apology. I make mistake of not seeing that possibility.''

"Hm,'' said Yake. "Out of the mouths of babes.''

"I must admit—'' said Madja, "it does not seem a very likely possibility to me, but it is the only possibility that we can accept that is not insulting to us—hmm? Is same problem, right? So! All right. Let us snatch victory from mouth of deceit, right? Right! If we solve it here, we solve it anywhere.'' She looked around the room for agreement.

Anne Larson nodded cautiously. Kasahara allowed himself a tiny smile of hope.

Yake thought about it for half a second, then looked Madja directly in the eyes. "Okay, right. Let's try it.'' He took a sip of his coffee. It was going to be a long night. He sighed and began: "Let me throw this out as a . . . a working assumption. A place to start from. What would an acceptable solution look like? What are the particles of it?''

"Honor," suggested Kasahara in a quiet voice. "It would have to be honorable."

Yake looked over at Nori, surprised. "I thought you were a pragmatist."

"I am. Honor is pragmatic."

"Hm. Okay. A solution has to be honorable. What else?"

Madja put up a finger. "I think solution must be fair. If it is not fair, one side or other will begin to resent it, question it, work against it. We have seen this in our own dealings."

"I can believe it," said Larson.

"I will ignore that one," said Madja, nonchalantly. "Coming as it does from the representative of senile colonialism."

"How kind of you," Larson smiled back.

"Let's stay on purpose," said Yake. "Anne, what about you?"

"I'm pragmatic." Larson pronounced her words carefully, and with a proper English accent. "I want it to be workable. We should be able to pay our debts without resentment or punishment. No human being should be hurt in the process or be forced to do anything that goes against his or her humanity. And yes, I'd like us to be able to keep our pride."

"Hm," said Yake. "Hm."

"Eh?" said Madja. "Is something wrong?"

"Not really. I was hoping for a little more agreement here."

Larson looked surprised. "I thought we were in agreement."

"You guys are, yes."

"Ah," said Madja. "What is it you are asking for, Yake? What would good solution look like to you?"

Yake said it flatly. "Revenge."

They blinked.

Yake spread his hands before him to show that he was hiding nothing. "I feel like I've been betrayed. I want to get even. Everything that each of you have said is absolutely correct and proper and appropriate and should be at the top of our list of criteria for an acceptable solution.

"But if we can have all that, and have an appropriate revenge, too, that's what I'd like."

Kasahara nodded politely. "I wouldn't object to that."

"Neither would I," agreed Larson.

"But of course," said Madja. "What good is solution if you can't also enjoy it?"

NO
SMALL
REWARD

Hnaxx reached across the intervening space and stroked the foreclaw of the young and lovely Rrr. "Thank you for a most enjoyable and successful mating," Hnaxx said. "Your enthusiasm and your delight are well appreciated. I shall reward you to the utmost should the larva prove healthy."

Rrr nodded its head in gentle acquiescence. It was still too young to talk with much fluency; it had eaten its way out of its own host-grub only a few seasons past.

Hnaxx let its claw linger on Rrr's for only a moment longer, then stood to address the rest of the gathering at the table.

"My lords and colleagues—" Hnaxx clacked its mandibles loudly for attention. The pavilion fell silent quickly as one green triangular head after another swiveled to that angle of the table. The large bright eyes all glittered like jewels.

"Let us honor the service that has been performed for us," Hnaxx began. "Let us honor with loud enthusiasm."

The room filled with the sound of clacking mandibles and rasping hindclaws, even a few delicious hoots as Hnaxx continued. "The young and clever K!rikkl has provided valuable information to this nest and we shall all prosper from it for many years. We are more than simply enriched. We are more than momentarily enriched. We shall ever be enriched by this service, both exemplary and extraordinary. Let us honor the one who has made it possible.

"Let us make K!rikkl one of us, flesh of our flesh, body of our body."

Hnaxx looked around the room at the other members of the powerful Trrrl^t nest. They were fat and juicy and their great multi-faceted eyes were focused like spotlights. "On your behalf, oh Noble Lords, the humble Hnaxx promised

K!rikkl that the nest stood ready to serve him—and tonight, we shall.''

Hnaxx clacked his foreclaws loudly.

Instantly, six sturdy servants strode into the room, carrying a great wooden platter upon which K!rikkl's body was cracked, pinioned, roasted, split, sauced, and sliced. The guests applauded enthusiastically, rattling their mandibles and rasping their hind legs loudly and vigorously.

"A great honor! A greaat honor!''.

"A beautiful feast! Bravo! Bravo!''

"How delicious the young Ki! looks!''

Hnaxx lowered itself next to Rrr again. "We shall impregnate many fine grubs, shall we not, my tenderness?''

Rrr rasped its claws demurely and labored to speak. "I stand ready to be mounted, my lord.''

"And so you shall. So you shall.''

Hnaxx turned to K!rikkl's steaming corpse in the center of the room and broke off the first tender leg. The juices dripped appetizingly from K!rikkl's foreclaws. Hnaxx felt gratified that the presumptuous, ill-mannered, ambitious and insulting young Ki! had met an appropriate fate. Delicately, Hnaxx cracked the shell of K!rikkl's claw and inserted its long yellow proboscis.

A moment of hesitation—

Yes.

K!rikkl was delicious.

Hnaxx stood up and announced, "The flesh is sweet! Let the feast begin!''

It was a grand evening! A grand evening indeed.

There would be much honor for the nest as a result of this evening. Indeed, three problems had been solved with one feast. What to do about K!rikkl, what to do about K!rikkl's grub—

And one other matter, which must be discussed privately with the Great Egg-Master.

Until then, of course, Hnaxx indulged most delightfully and enthusiastically in both of the major pleasures of the flesh. K!rikkl's and Rrr's.

Seldom was the resolution of an affair so satisfying.

* * *

The rest of the evening's entertainment proved equally successful.

Of course, the temperature songs and the orchard dances were a delight. They always were. As they wound to their inevitable and hilarious conclusions, many of the guests found themselves in extraordinarily revealing and indecent postures. Of course, they hurried to redress themselves, they always did; but there would be many embarrassing anecdotes to be told in the days to come.

After that, the pheromone sprays delighted almost everybody and even caused Old Yll!br to leap onto the table and attempt to mount what was left of K!rikkl's body in a (so Old Yll!br claimed) bawdy demonstration of northlander mating techniques. Of course, there were those who suggested otherwise, that this was not a demonstration of northlander mating techniques at all, that instead Old Yll!br had actually been overcome by the giddy sprays of hormonal influences. It sometimes happened in the elders, you know . . . when they reached that time of life.

But the big surprise of the evening was reserved for the darkness after the moons set. It happened when the guests began to filter out into the night to chew their aromatic herbs. Abruptly, there was a chorus of chirruping fanfare and the night was flooded with brilliant light of all colors.

Hnaxx had caused to be erected a huge tower of incandescent electric lights. They corruscated up and down through the entire visual spectrum; they glittered and flashed with brilliant intensity, illuminating the darkness with colors never before seen on this red-lit world. The guests all gasped with delight and horror. Their bright skins shone with multiple reflections that crawled across their carapaces like neon parasites. They stood and basked in the light and giggled with embarrassment at such juvenile displays of wonder.

The whole thing was terribly gaudy and obviously very expensive. The perfect delight. Beautiful and impressive both. The guests circled the tower in fascination. Several of the younger ones even tried to climb the tower; but it had been deliberately constructed to prevent them from climbing too far.

Even Hnaxx was surprised at the intensity of the delirium induced in the guests. The vendors had warned of this profound hypnotic effect, of course; but it was one thing to hear a fact and another to experience it. Indeed, Hnaxx found it quite difficult to resist the light itself. The urge to climb the tower was nearly irresistible.

Fortunately, Hnaxx had been warned of this phenomenon and had stayed a respectable distance away from the tower when it was illuminated. To some degree, this diluted the tropic power of the display. Without the warning, Hnaxx would have been as eager to succumb as the guests.

The off-world vendors had also warned not to leave the tower lights burning for too long, or it might risk burning out the eyes of the guests. Consequently, the machinery had been designed to flicker and flash for a short while only, and then gently fade to a quiescent glow and finally back to darkness. It could not be triggered a second time.

It was during the loudest part of this distraction that Hnaxx, obedient and honorable young Ki! that it was, reluctantly broke away and slipped quietly back into the festival pavilion where the Great Egg-Master waited patiently. The Egg-Master was still sitting impassively at the table.

Hnaxx approached on its belly, bowing its head to acknowledge the Master's great age and wisdom.

"You have done well, young Hnaxx."

"It is a privilege to serve the nest. I am grateful for the honor."

The Egg-Master blinked slowly and turned its head sideways to study Hnaxx. It swiveled its glittering multi-faceted eyes up and down as it focused. "You may speak."

"Thank you, my Master. I am pleased to report to you that the secret of the grubs is safe again, my lord. We have tracked down every one of those who came into possession of our sacred knowledge and dealt with them appropriately. K!rikkl was the last of the last who knew. Tonight, K!rikkl's debt to this nest has been well repaid."

"Indeed it has."

"I have not asked reward, Egg-Master. I never shall. It is reward enough to serve. Thank you for letting me have the honor of this duty. I stand forever ready to serve the Greater Trrrlˆt nest."

"You have done only what was expected of you, Hnaxx," whispered the Egg-Master. "That requires neither thanks nor acknowledgement. No reward could be asked in such a situation; and no reward shall be given. The only acknowledgement of your usefulness is that you shall continue to be used. But you understand that, of course." The Egg-Master rattled its mandibles and added, "There is still much to be done. May I speak plainly?"

"Master—?"

"We have not the time for the usual painless abstractions of courtesy; otherwise, your clever devices will not distract the guests long enough for us to say what we have to say to each other. Besides, the matter I would discuss with you is of such grave import that neither of us could risk the consequences of a communication that is less than precise. So I shall speak to you like a lover. Do you understand me, young Hnaxx?"

"I understand, my Master. I shall die before I compromise your candor."

"I expect nothing less. Now, listen to me carefully—for I must tell you of a matter that affects every Ki! alive today, and every Ki! that will ever follow after us."

Hnaxx wondered if it should prostrate itself before the seriousness of this topic, but the Egg-Master reached over and touched its foreclaw. "This is a great burden, young Hnaxx. We are indentured to our own history. And there is a price we are still paying for that indenture.

"This world is not fully our own. It was settled first by the Fnˆrr. They sought a new world, a warm land in which to nourish their roots, a place where their dreams would be peaceful and fat. They made a contract with the Dhrooughleem, the same aliens who sold you your pretty lights of distraction. It was a very expensive contract, but the Dhrooughleem promised to find a safe world for the Fnˆrr. They brought the Fnˆrr to this world, and the Fnˆrr were pleased. They found here a warm red light, which bathed them and made them strong; and they thought they had found paradise.

"But after the first few summers, as they began to spread their seeds, they began to discover that this paradise was infested by vermin, by brain-eating parasites that preyed upon them in their dream-time. They were horrified and enraged. As hard as it is to imagine one of the Fn^rr demonstrating any kind of emotion, they were hysterical with fear and anger. They had invested too much time and too many generations in this world, and now it had turned into a hellacious place of terror. The Fn^rr demanded that the Dhrooughleem make good on the original contract. The Dhrooughleem postulated what seemed to everyone a much better solution . . . symbiosis.

"We, the Ki!Lakken, were invited to share the expenses of colonizing this world. We would take a full third of the financial burden of the Fn^rr, and in return we would bring them protection and security.

"It should have been an ideal partnership, sweet Hnaxx. The Fn^rr-detested grubs are a tasty resource to us. Their flesh is sweet; their bodies are warm; we can plant our eggs in their bellies and watch our children grow large and healthy. So, the agreement was made and the slobbering off-worlders brought our ancestors here to this planet. The contract was simple. While the Fn^rr slept, we would care for their pavilions, we would eat the grubs, we would plant our eggs. During the summers, they are afoot and we are swarming. We would grow strong, the Fn^rr would grow strong. Only the grubs would suffer."

"Yes, my Master. And to all appearances, we have done that well."

"Too well. We have done well even beyond appearances. Do you know the rest of this contract?"

"No, my Master."

"The contract specifies that should either species fail to maintain its obligations to the Dhrooughleem, the other species shall come into full possession of the world. That is why we have never pushed the grubs to the edge of extinction. Should the grubs no longer molest the wandering plants, the Fn^rr would spread across our swarming grounds and in a very short time we would follow the vermin into blissful extinction.''

"The Fn^rr would not be so despicable as to break an agreement, my Master—would they?''

"Would *you* take such a chance with the future of *your* species? Neither would I. And neither would any other Ki!Lakken.'' The Egg-Master stroked Hnaxx's forelimb gently. "Indeed, it has been my own fondest hope that the vermin would continue to molest the Fn^rr in such great numbers that they themselves might be pushed up to their threshold of failure. Have you yourself not entertained such fantasies?''

"I confess that I do sometimes fall prey to such delusions, Master. They are occasionally delightful.''

The Egg-Master clacked its mandibles in soft delight. "You share the ambition of your nest. A commendable trait.

"It is true that we have been on this world for only a very few generations; still we have done much that we can be proud of. We have established many fine plantations and we have watched the grubs well. We have indentured many trustworthy servants—and the ones who have not been trustworthy have not remained in our indenture for long . . . as you well know. You have cleaned up their indiscretions and we have picked the bones of their children.

"Hnaxx, we have captured many grubs; we have raised them and learned how to breed many more. We have buried long years learning how to teach them well. We have taught them to forage. We have taught them what to eat and what not to eat. We have shown them what grows back and what does not. We should be seeing the fruits of these labors, and yet . . . every season there are more and more of the Fn^rr awakening from the dreams and walking into summer.''

"They see the future, my Master. They plant to meet the sun and the rain. They root in warm soil. They spread their seeds in too many places.''

"If only it were that simple, my child. They see the future, yes, and therein lies the seed of our failure. They see the unborn grubs. The visions trouble them. The more grubs they see, the more deaths they dream, the more they are troubled, then the more seeds they spread. We cannot breed the grubs as fast as they can spread their seeds. Now, despite the predations of the terrible vermin, they still spread into our swarming grounds. I begin to think—and I say this with only the greatest reluctance—that they do it deliberately."

"They plot our extinction?!!"

"So it would seem."

"I cannot imagine a species being so . . . so malevolent!"

"Perhaps they feel they no longer want to share their world with us. This was their world alone in the not-too-distant past. Perhaps they wish to return to that time of sole burden. Perhaps they feel we have not protected them well enough. . . . Whatever the case, we must consider new possibilities now. And you, dear Hnaxx, must be part of those possibilities."

"Whatever I can do, my lord."

"And so you shall. Here is a conundrum for you to consider. Tell me what you see in this circumstance."

"Yes, my lord."

"We have been approached by the Dhrooughleem again. They are concerned for us. They see our discomfort; they wish to offer aid. They have suggested that we might wish to increase our supply of these grubs—strictly as food and larval incubators, of course—but they suggest most politely that they might be in a position to supply some very large numbers of grubs in the near future."

"That *is* an interesting conundrum," remarked Hnaxx.

"Indeed, it is." The Egg-Master's eyes glittered with the reflections of many small lamps. "What do you see in it?"

"I see one possibility, my lord. It is a possibility that can be seen only by one possessed of certain experience—but because I am the one with that experience, I do see this way."

"Speak, Hnaxx."

"It is this, my Master. K!rikkl's grub was too well trained. It spoke. It demonstrated that it could reason. The thought that it suggests, my Father, is that the grubs may be far more intelligent than ever we suspected. Perhaps even they may be a . . ." Hnaxx lowered its head ashamedly. "I apologize in advance for what I am about to suggest, my Father. It is shameful and degrading. But I must say it here in the hope that I am wrong, rather than risk someone else saying it in the Forum and being proven right."

"Go on," encouraged the Egg-Master.

"Yes, my Father. The thought occurs to me that the grubs may be members of an intelligent species. Perhaps, even, they are members of a species that belongs to the Inter-Change. If such were so—and if such were to be discovered and made public—then we would be guilty of the most heinous crime of *Involuntary Subjugation.* Our people could be liable to a permanent indenture. We would lose our freedom and our world. Forgive me, my lord, but I must speak this possibility in the hopes that you will tell me that I am dreadfully mistaken."

The Egg-Master did not contradict Hnaxx—and that was the most terrifying thing that Hnaxx had ever heard: the silence of the Father.

Hnaxx said simply, "Ai-eee. We are doomed then, are we not?"

The Egg-Master lowered its head. "It is a curious puzzle—but as the pieces fall into place, the puzzle becomes less puzzling. I wonder, who are these grubs we use for food and larval incubators?"

"Perhaps the Dhroo might know—?"

"Indeed, they must! But, Hnaxx? You are not so innocent as to think that the Dhroo are themselves so blameless in the matter? Indeed, it was the Dhroo who first suggested to our ancestors that, if we were unable to protect the Fn^rr, then they might be unable to meet their obligations elsewhere, and if that situation came to pass then our people would inherit sole custody of this world. We believed the Dhroo then. Now we find that the Dhroo have outplayed our hand in this cycle of the game. Should we believe them again?"

"Never, my Master. We should pour salt on the Dhroo!"

"We will have to live long enough first. The Dhroo know

what they have done to us. They know what is in our egg
pouch, Hnaxx! Because they put it there! There is a hungry
Knrkt sleeping in our nest and very soon it will awaken. It
seems to me that it is only a matter of time before the
terrible truth is known and we shall be punished for our
cleverness.''

"My Father, let me be impudent." Hanxx raised up and
looked directly into the elder's eyes. "Is it not still possible
that we can complete this cycle without discovery? If we
were somehow able to celebrate a conclusion, we would
have nullified the trap, would we not? In such a case, we
could only be acknowledged for our cleverness rather than
be punished for our crime. Such is the way the game is
played. I urge you, let me look for such a solution. Let me
serve the nest. Let me serve the world.''

The Egg-Master nodded thoughtfully, rasping its mandibles in agreement. "I had hoped you would be bold enough
for such a duty, my child, my little one; but there is one
way immediately in which such a responsibility could be
granted—''

"My lord?''

The old one was silent for a long moment. "Your nest
would have to carry a terrible burden on behalf of the Father
of All Nests. Should you fail, it would mean the dissolution
of your nest and the deaths of all the nestlings. Are you
prepared to accept such a responsibility?''

"My Father, it would be only an honor. What is thy
charge?''

"Should we fail to complete this cycle of the game,
should this terrible secret become known, then your nest—
the whole of it and every member—shall have to step
forward to claim the honor of gracing the table at the
InterChange. Do you understand?''

Hnaxx bowed its head. "My Father, I understand
completely. If there is a victory here, then it is a victory for
all and I will have no claim on any part of it. If there is a
failure though, it shall be my nest's failure and ours alone—
and none of it may be laid upon the table of any other Ki!.

My Master, I have already accepted this honor by virtue of being your child.''

The old one clacked its mandibles appreciatively and reached out to stroke Hnaxx's foreclaw. ''You are a treasure, my pretty little one. Would you like to be mounted tonight?''

''Whatever pleases you, my lord.''

A
SMALL
PROMOTION

Yake Singh Browne thought about it for as long as he could, then decided it was best not to think about it at all.

He swallowed hard, thought about it for the thirty-third time, decided that there was no other way, gritted his teeth, and put in his application for an audience with an Oracle.

The T'ranian Oracle.

But he didn't expect it to be approved.

The High Council of the InterChange was comprised of the representatives of the seventeen most successful—and oldest—species in the known galaxy. The members of the High Council were called Oracles. They were charged with the responsibility of advising the various species of the InterChange in any way they felt appropriate.

Sometimes their advice could be extraordinarily valuable. And just as often, it could prove utterly worthless. Nevertheless, the price was the same regardless of the answers given: if you have to ask, you can't afford it.

The most expensive Oracle of all was the T'ranian Oracle.

Also known as . . . *The Dragon.*

The Dragons were the oldest and most successful member species in InterChange history. The Dragons had personally retired over three hundred and twelve other species.

No, Yake did not expect the application to be approved.

There were species in the InterChange that no human being had ever had contact with. Over two thousand species were registered. (More than six thousand species were known, but many of those were fortunately unable to afford membership.) Humans had met (and exchanged greetings with) one hundred and thirteen alien races. Of those one hundred and thirteen, the sons and daughters of Terra had been able to open diplomatic negotiations with nine.

It was understandable, of course.

91

Human beings smelled bad. And tasted worse.

Of the two-thousand-plus species in the InterChange, only a small minority was mammalian, and so far the statistical evidence suggested that the universe was indeed set up to generate intelligent mammalian life only as the very rare exception to the way things were *supposed* to work. Most of the alien races in the galaxy had evolved from the equivalent of insects, reptiles, dinosaurs, sea-dwellers, and occasionally plants—cabbages, to be exact. On most of the worlds of the galaxy, mammal-like creatures never got the chance to come down from the trees or out of their burrows. The greatest majority of species in the InterChange were reptilian, followed by the insect-evolved and the sea-dwellers. To most of those races, mammals were . . . food. Or incubators. Or just plain vermin.

Yake was just about certain that his petition would be rejected.

("Guess what wants to join the InterChange! No, don't bother, you'll never guess. You're not going to believe this, Fzour'sx. *Mammals!* No, I am not pulling your gzornty. I saw them myselves. Real mammals! Yes! And they're just intelligent enough to understand the concept of intelligence! They *claim* that entitles them! Well, I know! But can you *believe* the presumption? No, no—wait, it gets better. The way I hear it, Fzour'sx, there was this comet that smacked into their world, and the resulting ice age killed off all the dinosaurs just when they had reached the threshold of sentience. Of course, it'd be a tragedy, if it weren't so *bizarre*. It was an ecological vacuum; the mammals began to evolve like fruit flies—the nasty little egg-suckers grabbed all the good ecological niches for themselves and the reptiles never got the chance to regroup. I mean, talk about your ecological opportunists! What's that? How do they taste? I don't know yet. Gxammel is planning a festival, so maybe we'll find out then. I'm not so sure that I want to. The way I hear it, on their planet—*the mammals feed on the birds!*")

Of course, there was no such thing as species prejudice. Not in the InterChange. It was just that . . . well, few races felt comfortable speaking to something that looked as if it belonged on a plate.

No human being had ever had an audience with a Dragon before. And Yake did not expect to be the first.

And then the Ambassador asked him to step into his office.

When Yake entered, the Old Man was holding a copy of the application. "This is going to be very expensive, Yake," was the Ambassador's only comment.

"Did you want me to withdraw the petition?"

The Ambassador shook his head. "No, it's too late for that. We've already been charged the application fee. Even if we withdraw the petition, we still have to pay the fee."

The Old Man turned to stare out the window at the steep wall of cliffs opposite. The InterChange world was carved with rugged canyons so deep that you couldn't see the bottoms. Below a certain depth, it was a world of perpetual night. Outside the window, the twilight canyons were haloed in curtains of glittering light. "I assume it's necessary, Yake, or you wouldn't have put in the request. It's just that . . ." He trailed off thoughtfully.

"Sir?"

The Ambassador sighed. "It's the cost. I can't help thinking—wondering—how many human beings are going to have to work for how many years to pay for this application if you're wrong. I can't help wondering what kind of jobs they'll have to do." The Ambassador looked very unhappy. "You do know, of course, how we are viewed by the other races here, Yake?"

"Yes, sir."

"I can't begrudge you the effort, Yake. You have to do your job. But please—remember who has to pay the bill when it comes due."

"Yes, sir."

"Now, then—" The Ambassador cleared his throat. "About your request—"

"Yes, sir?"

"It's been refused."

"Oh. Well. . . ." Yake wasn't surprised.

"The T'ranian Oracle never speaks to anyone below the status of Ambassadorial Delegate."

"Oh. Well . . . it seemed like a good idea at the time." Yake sighed—*well, he'd expected the petition to be rejected, so why was he so disappointed?!!* He sighed again and turned to go. "Okay, we'll go to Plan B."

"Wait a minute, Yake."

"Sir?"

The Ambassador turned around to face him. "Yake, I hope you're right."

"Sir?"

"About the Dragons. I signed your promotion papers two days ago and resubmitted the application. It was approved this morning."

For a moment, Yake didn't have the words to reply. "Uh—thank you, sir."

"Don't thank me, Yake. Just be right. Your appointment is in an hour and a half. You'll just have time to get suited. I took the liberty of ordering a new uniform for you. Stripes, insignia, boots—everything. Wear it all. Even the sword. We've even had the translator repaired."

"Yes, sir! Thank you, sir." Yake turned to go, then stopped. "Uh, sir—just one question. This promotion—it's only for the purpose of speaking to the Oracle, right?"

"Of course not! It's a full promotion. Full salary, all the perks. Even your own parking place. No matter what happens in your interview with the Oracle, you'll *keep* your promotion."

"Uh, thank you, sir. But, uh—if the request hadn't been granted—?"

"Yake, don't ask stupid questions. And don't keep the Oracle waiting, either. And oh, yes, in case I don't get a chance to tell you later, congratulations."

"In case you don't get a—uh, right. Uh, thank you, sir."

"Don't thank me, Yake."

"Sir?"

The Ambassador looked unhappy. "Go on, now. It's late. You'd better get going."

"Yes, sir!"

CHESS
WITH
THE
DRAGON

Never play chess with a Dragon.

Especially not if the Dragon is the size of a house and has teeth longer than your arm.

This was common wisdom. You did not need to be a member of the InterChange to understand why.

On the other hand (as they say), if you have nothing to lose . . . you can always lose your other hand.

Yake felt intimidated.

He approached as close as he dared—but even from this distance, the Dragon was . . . well, *intimidating*.

The Dragon was resting on a small hill; it looked bored. It was hard to tell. How do you read an expression that's as wide as a billboard?

"Ahem. . . ." Yake began hesitantly.

The Dragon looked up.

Yake blanched.

The creature was green; so green it looked like an anomaly in the air. Its scales shone like polished metal, a shimmering verdant nightmare. Its eyes were as large as windows, and they were the brightest shade of searing red. They looked as if they were lit from within.

The Dragon's mouth—Yake swallowed hard—its mouth was the door into deepest hell. The Dragon's breath was so hot, Yake could feel it from here. It felt like a blast furnace! Only not as refreshing.

Yake took an involuntary step back; then he realized how that must look and forced himself to take a step forward again. "I'm Yake Singh Browne. The Terran Delegate."

"Yesss, you are," said the Dragon.

"Yes, I am," said Yake. (He looked at the sky. Oh, God, did I just say that? Lord, please don't let me be too big a fool here today.)

"You have questions?" The Dragon asked drily. It turned one great blazing eye toward Yake.

"Many questions, yes."

"Are they interesting questionsss . . . ?"

"I suppose it depends on what you would call interesting."

"Survival is often interesting—isss it not?"

Yake thought about it. Sometimes survival demanded all of your attention. By that definition—"Yes, survival is very interesting."

"Yesss, but only when it's your own. Then it's interesting. When it is not your own survival that is being discussed, it is not a matter of interest at all, is it? So I will ask again. These questions that you intend to ask, are they questions that I will find interesting?"

"Uh, no. Um—at least, I don't think so."

"Then why should I answer them? Perhaps I should ask you an interesting question?"

"Um . . . perhaps we could *trade* questions."

"Trade *questions?"* The Dragon looked as if it wanted to raise an eyebrow.

"Well, uh—it's a game we play on my planet. I show you mine, you show me yours."

"But I am not interested in seeing yours."

"Oh. Well. Um. Er. Okay. May I ask you a small question anyway? A question of no importance."

"Yesss?"

"Why do they say . . . 'Never play chess with a Dragon?' "

"Yesss, a small question of no importance. Perhaps . . . it is because of the tradition."

"The tradition?"

"The tradition that the winner gets to eat the loser."

"I see." Yake smiled nervously. He wondered if he should declare his intentions as peaceful. "I have no intention of eating you," he offered.

"I know that, yesss." The Dragon smiled. The effect was ghastly. *"The converse, however, is not true."*

"Uh. Yes. Thank you. I think."

"You have other questionsss?" The Dragon swung its head around expectantly. Yake jumped back in surprise.

"Uh, yes, I do. Have other questions, that is. Maybe they could be interesting to you, maybe not. Um, you know who we are, don't you?"

"Yesss. We call you the—the—excuse me, the word does not translate. We call you 'the presumptuous food.' "

"Yes, of course. We understand our uniqueness in the universe. But let me ask you this: isn't it of some interest to you to know how we got here? How mammals became intelligent on our world instead of insects or reptiles?"

The Dragon did not even consider it. *"No,"* it rumbled. *"The galaxy is big. Accidents happen. If that is all you wish to discuss, then this shall be a very disappointing afternoon, indeed."* The Oracle began to raise itself up on its forward legs. Yake could see the ground sagging beneath its weight. *"At least, I shall have the minor satisfaction of discovering if you are enjoyable food or not."*

"Sir—" Yake wondered if the term were correct. Never mind. He spoke quickly. "There is another question I want to ask, a much more important question—a very *interesting* question. I mean, interesting to my species at least."

"At least, yesss." The Dragon paused. *"Go on."*

"It's the indenture—I mean, our debt. We uh, we think we've been slimed."

"Ssslimed?"

"Suckered. Played for fools. Cheated. By the Dhroo."

"Ahh, yesss. The Dhroo." The Dragon chewed over the thought with relish. *"Yesss. A not unfamiliar circumstance. And you wish an ansssswer, yesss?"*

"Uh, no. Not exactly. Um, we're really not able to pay in the currency that you're most likely to request."

"An asssumption, but not a stupid one. Mammalsss. . . ." sighed the Dragon. *"You think with your glands. Well, then . . . what are you assking?"*

"We can't afford to buy your help. And we're not asking you for a solution, because we can't afford to pay you for it. Nor can we ask you for your advice, because we can't afford that either. No. What I want to ask is much smaller."

"Yesss?"

"I want to ask if something is possible."

"You ask about . . . survival? Survival is always a possibility. So is the alternative."

"No. We already know that. What I want to know is—I mean, if this is a game—then so far, it's been a very interesting game for my species. Very interesting. What I want to know is this: is there a way to make the game equally interesting for the Dhroo?"

"Ahhh," said the Dragon. *"A fine question. A very fine question."* It lowered itself back down to the ground and ruminated for a moment. It rumbled deep in its throat, a loud purring noise like the sound of an ancient subway train roaring through an underground tunnel.

Yake waited patiently.

At last, the Dragon looked up. *"Yesss, there is a way."*

Yake waited for the Dragon to go on. The Dragon quietly returned his gaze.

"You are waiting for something else?"

"You said there's a way?"

"Yesss. There is. You were waiting for a hint, perhaps? It is too bad that you cannot afford to ask the question outright. But the price that we would require . . . you are better off not knowing." The Dragon smiled broadly. Yake nearly fainted.

"Perhaps—" continued the Dragon, *"—you should consider this an opportunity to demonstrate the intelligence of your species. Knowing that there is a possibility should be a goad to guarantee its discovery. And if you cannot discover the answer, then that, too, is an answer."*

Yake pursed his lips, holding in the first reply that came to his mind. Instead, he nodded politely. "You have done us a great service."

"Perhapsss. And perhapsss not. Consider this: Losing a game is one thing; you can be eaten knowing that you have done your best. But losing a game when you know that there is a solution that you have not found is intolerable, because it suggests that even your best was not good enough. This

might be a more expensive answer than you bargained for, little snack."

"I'll—we'll take that chance."

"Yesss, you will."

"Is there anything else that you can tell us?"

"There is quite a bit that I can tell you. But I won't. It is not interesting enough." The Dragon paused, then it raised its head up and looked at Yake. *"I will not eat you today, Yake Singh Browne. And perhapsss I will not eat you the next time either."*

"The next—" Yake gulped, "—time?"

"Yesss." The Dragon lashed its tail around itself and looked directly at Yake. *"The price that I require for this discussion is this: you must come back and tell me how you work it all out."* It added, *"That is . . . if you do."*

"Thank you. Sir." Yake began to back away.

The Dragon lowered its head again and appeared to go to sleep. *"Don't . . . thank . . . me. . . ."*

"Yes, sir!"

Yake's heart rate did not return to normal for two days.

A
GLASS
OF
BHEER

The hour was tired and Yake was late. "The late Yake Singh Browne," he muttered and sipped at his bheer. He made a face and put the glass back on the table in front of him.

"Soon we will all be late," agreed Madja.

"You can put it on my tombstone," said Anne Larson, brushing her graying hair back off her forehead. "Better late than never." She giggled at the joke.

Yake looked across at her. "I think you've had enough for tonight, Anne."

She hiccuped and giggled again.

Yake and Madja, Anne and Nori were the only four people left in the lounge. They all looked haggard.

They had been sitting there and arguing for hours. Perhaps for days. No one remembered.

The argument was a peripatetic orangutan, bouncing off the walls of their separate frustrations like a ping-pong ball in a wind tunnel. The mere knowledge that an answer was possible was like a goad.

Only . . . Yake was tired of being goaded. He wanted to experience a result once in awhile, too.

He stared into his bheer unhappily. "I'd rather have beer," he said. "I'm tired of the sacred 'H'. I'm tired of alcoholh."

Madja agreed with a sour nod. "Is same for me, but right now, I would just as happily settle for one straight answer."

"You have one straight answer. The Dragon says mate in four moves *is* possible."

"It did not say how. Is like famous story about Borozinsky—greatest chess player of his century—he drove opponent crazy this way. He said, 'If you were any good, you would see that mate is possible in four moves and

105

resign.' Was no mate possible, but opponent died in frustration rather than admit he could not find it.''

"Hmm," said Yake. "Chess players can be nasty."

"Yah. Too bad this is not chess," agreed Madja. "Chess, I could defeat a whole herd of Dragons."

"Yeah, and then you'd have to eat them," put in Larson, giggling. She looked positively tipsy.

Madja frowned at her. "That would be easy part. I share them with you. But, no. This is not chess. This is—more like American game. Too much free-for-all. Not enough discipline. How can anyone play game that is all lies?"

Yake looked up at her blearily. "What?"

"Is not important. Was nasty shot."

"Cheap shot. Never mind. Say it again."

Madja shrugged. "I said, 'Is not chess. Is American game. Too much free-for-all.' " She sipped at her vhodka.

"No, you said something else—"

She waved a hand. "That was nasty part: 'How can anyone play game that is all lies?' "

"You're right, Madja! That *is* an American game. This isn't chess! This is poker!"

"Polka?"

"Poker," said Kasahara. "You know? The card game."

"Ahh, yes!" Madja grinned and said something in Russian.

"They teach you that in the Navy?" asked Yake.

"Among other things, *da.*"

"I don't know whether to be impressed or shocked."

"You learn to poker. I learn to swear. Which is more useful?"

"Right now? Poker."

Madja looked uninterested.

"Okay," said Yake. "Maybe I'm wrong, but try this thought on anyway. This is a poker game—with two thousand sharpies, each of whom has brought his own deck and his own set of rules! Do you know what that means?"

"You are about to explain it, no?"

"It means that there are no rules. Only there are! But we

get to make them up as we go! That's how this game is played. Do you know what a good poker game needs?''

"Good players?" asked Larson.

"Nah. A fish. A sucker. Somebody with money who's willing to believe whatever you tell him—especially when you tell him that you couldn't possibly have the fourth ace, because you want to keep him in the game as long as he has money to lose. That's us—we're the poor fish in this game! Humanity! We're the suckers! As long as we're playing by their rules, we have to lose. It's their game! We can't win unless we change the rules on them—''

"Yake," Madja chose her words carefully. "I do not understand what you are saying. It sounds like you are suggesting that we break agreements here."

"No—I'm not. I'm suggesting that we . . . reinterpret the boundaries of those agreements to include the possibility that we could win a hand here, too."

Madja did not look convinced.

"You don't understand, do you? This isn't a game about playing by the rules. It's a game about how cleverly you can cheat. If that's the game, then cheating isn't wrong, is it?''

"Is interesting capitalist justification. Do they teach that at UCLA?''

"USC. And I didn't go there. Never mind. I just want to make this game a little less interesting for us and a little more interesting for everybody else."

"I do not see it, Yake."

Larson leaned across the table and laid one hand on Madja's. "Think of it this way, dear. *Everything* is justified in the class struggle against the imperialist war-mongers."

"Is not good comparison, Larson. I am not sure that these creatures are really imperialists. Besides, imperialists on Earth are at least human. Theory is that human beings should *know better.* In the act of oppressing the class struggle of the workers, they renounce the noblest part of their humanity and deserve to meet their fate on the gallows. But Dragons and slugs and talking turnips might not be capable of knowing better. In that case, we cannot take advantage of them—*or we would be the oppressor.*"

Kasahara paused in the act of reheating his sahke. "Are you sure you're a real Communist?"

"I show you my card," said Madja, standing up and unbuttoning her blouse pocket. "I carry it everywhere I go."

"Never mind," interrupted Yake. "We're off the track. Madja, maybe this is only a game to the other species because they don't have as much at stake—but you're the one who pointed out that the stakes in this game are human dignity. Maybe this game is about measuring your dignity by how clever you are, not by how honorable. Maybe honor is the booby prize."

"I had not thought of that," Madja admitted. She fell silent. She looked sad at the idea, and for a moment even Yake felt sorry for her. She looked so . . . vulnerable. Abruptly, she looked up. "Is one thing wrong, Yake."

For just a moment, Yake hoped she was right. "Yes?"

"Is assumption you are making here about InterChange. You keep saying is game. Is clever. Is very American clever. But is maybe sacrifice truth for clever, Yake. For one hundred and sixty-seven years, we have known what InterChange was—interstellar government, no? Now you are saying it is not?"

Yake said, a little too quickly, "Maybe that hundred and sixty-seven years was the false assumption—" and immediately wished he hadn't said it.

Madja took it seriously. The color was draining from her face.

"You are right, Yake," she said finally. "We must question everything." She looked to Yake again. "But if we question everything must we question if game analogy is also accurate?"

"I think that's what we have to find out."

Kasahara said softly, "We're going to have to make some very hard assumptions here."

Larson turned to him and asked, "Nori, tell me something. What do you do if you're losing a game?"

Nori shrugged. "I pay my debts and go home."

"We can't do that here. What else can you do?"

"I don't know poker that well." Nori looked up. "Yake is the expert. What do you do?"

Larson shrugged. "I don't know either. I'm no expert in game theory."

"Forget game theory. I'll tell you what I'd do." Yake leaned back in his chair and put his feet up on the table. "I'd bring in the pros from Dover and kick some assets."

"The what?"

"The 'pros from Dover.' It's an American expression. It means—you bring in the power hitters. Um—you call for an expert."

"There are no experts here," moaned Madja. "Just capitalists. That is what makes the whole thing so *dreary*."

"Then we'll bring in an expert capitalist—" Yake said, and then caught himself in surprise. "My God! That's it!" He turned excitedly to Kasahara. "Warm up your keyboard, Nori! I want you to download a complete set of—no, wait. Limit your search to mammalian species only. Which species has been the most successful overall in its transactions with the InterChange?"

"Don't bother, Nori," said Anne. "Yake, I can tell you without looking. It's the Rh/attes."

"The rats?"

"The Rh/attes. The '/' is silent." Larson grinned. "They're the ones who want to indenture themselves to us."

"Oh, right."

"I've been doing some research. The Rh/attes are so successful that *nobody* trusts them."

"Oh, that's terrific," said Madja. "Capitalist pigs."

"No, Rh/attes."

"Is no difference."

"Wait a minute—" said Yake. "I don't care if they're dancing bears, if they're successful! What's the gimmick, Anne? How are they doing it?"

"I think—that they're uh, there's no polite word for it. They're 'snitches.' "

"Snitches?" asked Madja. "What is 'snitches'?"

"It's an American word," said Larson. "It means Supreme Hero of the Soviet Republic."

"Oh," said Madja. And then frowned, as much in puzzlement as in anger.

"They're spies," said Yake. "Right?"

"Mmmm." Larson made a face. "Not quite. That's one of their services. Information management. Nobody wants to issue a warrant of foreclosure on them because they're too valuable as snitches. And besides, nobody is sure what secrets they'd accidentally let drop about the species who signed the warrant."

"Nice position to be in," said Yake.

"How did Rh/attes get this way?" asked Madja.

"Apparently," said Nori, studying the screen of his clipboard, "they have the nasty habit of indenturing themselves to anyone who'll take them on."

"Interesting. What happens to the species that do?"

"Apparently, they benefit." Nori hesitated, then added, "Well, most of them, anyway." He peered at his screen with a frown. "Apparently, there were a couple that didn't."

"Were?"

"Maybe I don't understand the reference. It just says here, 'retired.'"

Yake sipped his bheer and thought for a moment. He looked across the table at his colleagues. "Well. Okay. It looks like there are risks involved here, too."

Larson said, "I don't think we have any choice. I vote yes."

Madja sighed and said, "Of course, I must officially protest dealing with capitalist swine like Rh/attes."

Yake looked over at her. "And off the record?"

"Off the record? Off the record, I am very curious and will allow myself to be outvoted."

"Nori?"

"My grandfather was a capitalist." Nori grinned broadly. "I'll take the chance."

"Good. Then it's three yes and one abstention. We talk to the Rh/attes."

"First, we have another dhrink—" said Larson. "We're going to nheed it."

A
GAME
OF
RH/ATTES
AND
DRAGONS

The Rh/attes were as unsavory as their name suggested.

They smelled musty—like old hair. Like old cheese. Like mildew.

The Rh/attes were dark and sinister creatures only chest-high to a man. They had little, malicious eyes and stood hunched forward, like crones over a cauldron, rubbing and twisting their ugly bony fingers in a continual wringing motion. To make it worse, they wore coarse black capes with hoods that made them look like assistants to Death. Their eyes gleamed red in the shadowed cowls—but not the searing red of the Dragon's eyes, no; the Rh/attes' eyes were embers, like smoldering coal.

Yake could see just far enough within their hoods to tell that they had coarse black fur and round pink ears that lay flat against the sides of their narrow heads.

They had yellow-stained teeth.

And they hissed and sprayed spittle when they spoke.

Yake tried not to think about the comparisons, but it was impossible. He couldn't help but think of these creatures as . . . well, *rats*.

There were six of them. They sniffed the air and eyed the humans suspiciously.

The four humans sat on chairs facing the six Rh/attes. The Rh/attes curled their naked gray tails around them and sat on their haunches.

Yake swallowed hard and looked at his colleagues. Madja looked a little gray. Anne Larson was expressionless. Kasahara's eyes were narrowed and his jaw was tight.

At last, one of the Rh/attes spoke. Its voice squeaked like a rusty gate. "You are stupid very species," it said. "Mammaloids have time enough hard in the universe. Not have to make it worse for us, the rest."

113

Yake thought about an appropriate response. He discarded
the first two things that came to his mind and chose the rest
of his words carefully. He looked to the others, then turned
back to the first Rh/atte. "We also find your species
disgusting. You remind us of the vermin of our own world.
Do you also spread disease and parasites wherever you go?"

Larson looked at Yake, astonished. Madja Poparov's head
snapped around so fast, Yake was surprised it didn't come
off. "Yake!" For a moment, even Kasahara lost his inscrut-
ability. Yake ignored all three of them.

"Good!" The Rh/atte grinned. "Understand we each
other." Its grin was disgusting.

"Yes, we do," said Yake. "We know who you are and
what you are. So we would prefer not to waste time on false
performances of courtesy and friendship."

"Slugs you have been talking to, yes? Dhrooughleem?
Yes? One hundred and twenty-three ritual ways to commit
copulatory obscenities, yes?"

"Yes and yes," said Yake. "Tell me, how many ways
do the Rh/attes commit copulatory obscenities?"

"Is price to pay for that information," said another of the
Rh/attes. Its eyes were narrow and flat.

"Yake!" whispered Madja angrily. "What do you say?"

"Shut up," Yake snapped back. He turned back to the
Rh/attes. "I am Yake Singh Browne. I would deal with you
on behalf of my species. Will you deal with me?"

"How bold you are," said the second Rh/atte. "Particularly now when your species has one foot in Dragon's
mouth and the other in slime."

"Do you want to trade information or insults? If you want
to trade insults, I'm afraid you will find that your species is
hopelessly inadequate to the task. You don't have the brains
to be insulted."

"Not bad," said a third Rh/atte. "Not bad at all—for
amateur one."

Yake stood up. "Let's go," he said to his colleagues. "I
have better things to do than listen to the droolings of
pretentious vermin."

"Wait—!" said a fourth Rh/atte. "Proposal, we listen."

"Proposal, *you* offer," retorted Yake. "You are the ones who asked to indenture yourselves to us. Why?"

"Why not?" the fifth Rh/atte answered. "If win you, win we. If lose you, still win we."

"What's to keep us from selling you as food or larval incubators or bio-sites for bacteriological and viral colonies?"

The Rh/atte smiled. "Thinking are you of our albino cousins. Useful are they very for those purposes. We are not."

"I see. So, what you're saying is that the Rh/attes are not much use for anything, are you?"

"Some species think that. Some species are retired, yes?"

"Yes, I've heard that." Yake looked at the Rh/attes. "We have no intention of being retired."

"And if retired you are, then know will we that you have changed mind, yes again?"

Yake didn't answer that. He thought frantically for a moment, then turned back to the Rh/attes again. "All right, let me come right out and ask it. Exactly what advantage could we gain if we were to accept your indenture?"

"None at all. None at all."

"So then, why should we accept your offer? Why should we enter into this deal? You offer no benefit to us."

"Benefit not is not to you. It is to us." That was the sixth and final Rh/atte. "Offer benefit us and we not need this indenture."

Yake stared at it.

The Rh/atte met his gaze with quiet rheumy eyes.

"Understand you? Yes?" It asked.

"Understand I," Yake agreed. He turned to the others. "Do *you* understand what he's offering?"

"Is nothing offered, I see," said Madja.

"That's right. Is nothing offered."

Larson sniffed. "I'm with Madja. I'm confused."

"I am not confused. I just see nothing."

"Never mind—" interrupted Yake. "Nori?"

Kasahara shook his head slowly. "I don't get a read on this, Yake. It's your hunch."

"I want to be cautious," Yake whispered to his colleagues. "I really do. We got into this mess by *trusting* the damn Dhroo. But we can't afford to be cautious anymore." He turned back to the Rh/attes abruptly and said, "We don't believe in indentures. We want to try something different."

"Different?"

"Do you *trade* information?"

"*Trade* . . . information?" The Rh/attes all looked surprised.

"Yes," said Yake. "Trade."

"What advantage is in . . . trade?"

"The advantage in trade is that there is no disadvantage."

"Is our customary contract *not*."

"That's right. It's ours. We have a special contract for dealing with mammalian species. Don't you?"

The Rh/attes' whiskers twitched. They looked to each other, touching their cowls and chittering softly within the dark little cathedrals they formed.

At last, the Rh/attes turned forward again, and the sixth Rh/atte spoke simply. "Information you have. Information accept we gladly. Information we have. Information accept you gladly."

Yake exchanged glances with the others. They looked hopeful. Yake motioned them to keep quiet and turned back to the Rh/attes. "I have a question."

"Is?"

Even as he began to ask it, he already knew the answer. Why hadn't he seen this before? "You're working for the Dragons, aren't you?"

The Rh/attes merely stared at him. Finally, the first one said, "Is question with answer expensive, yes. And interesting too. Wish you to ask it?"

"No. No, thank you."

"So," said the first Rh/atte. "This is how trade works. Is works. Now ask we the question. Negotiations here are beginning or ending? Yes?"

"Beginning," said Yake. "You Rh/attes may be vermin, but you're *our* vermin."

"Mutual is feeling," agreed the Rh/attes.

THE
LIBRARIAN'S
NIGHTMARE

The Ambassador from Terra looked exhausted.

He looked old.

Not like the Old Man. But like an *old man*.

For the first time, Yake began to feel sorry for the strain he must be putting on his boss.

The Ambassador accepted Yake's report without expression. He laid the folder on his desk without looking at it.

"Is everything all right, sir?"

"As well as can be expected, I suppose," the Ambassador said. "I haven't been sleeping well, Yake. I don't think you understand the size of the bills that you and your committee have been running up." He massaged the knuckles of his hand as if merely to move caused him pain. "What are you downloading, anyway?"

Yake had expected this question. He was prepared. "Sir, at the suggestion of the Rh/attes, we're doing some research into the past five hundred years of treaties and negotiations in which the Dhroo have participated."

"Mm, yes," said the Ambassador. "I don't suppose I can argue with that; but you are turning into a very interesting problem, Yake. You're either going to be the greatest hero in history—or the greatest incompetent. And I'm the guy who has to give you enough rope so we can find out which. I would feel much better if you had some *tangible* results to report."

"Yes, sir. Uh, we have found one thing; but you're not going to like it very much."

The Ambassador sighed. He straightened himself and faced the younger man. "I can handle it, Yake. Go on."

"Well . . . it's the InterChange, sir. Um . . . we thought it was a—a cross between a federation and a library. A place

119

where species could exchange information about each other.''

"It's not?"

"No, sir. It's not. We were wrong about the governmental functions of the InterChange. It's not a government at all. It never was intended to be. It's a—'' Yake looked embarrassed. He looked at his feet. ''We should have figured it out a long time ago, but we just kept assuming that the old assumptions were true because nobody ever questioned them. The, um—the InterChange is really a—a gigantic Monopoly game. A kind of a cross between a poker club and a pyramid scheme.

"You see, we thought that we were buying the book of the month from an interstellar library—that was what the Dhroo suggested—so we just kept downloading it as fast as we could, everything there was to know about all the other important species. Those other species knew better. We were buying poker chips! Information to use in the game! *Against them!* So they're all suspicious of us. We have no friends in this universe, sir.''

The Ambassador sank down into his chair. He looked ashen. ''That *is* bad news, Yake.''

"No, sir. That's not the bad news. This is—''

"It gets worse??!!''

"Sir? Are you all right?''

"I will be. Give me a moment.'' The Ambassador slipped two small pills into his mouth and took a drink of water. He coughed into his handkerchief for a moment, then looked to Yake again.

"Sir, if you'd rather—''

"No. I'd *rather* go to the gallows with my eyes open, Yake. Tell me the rest.''

"Yes, sir. It's this. No matter how bad you think it's been—well, it's worse than that. We've also been wrong about the library part.''

The last of the color drained from the Ambassador's face.

"Sir? Do you want me to call the doctor—?''

"No, no—please, go on.''

"Sir, I really—''

"Yake!"

"Yes, sir. Well, uh—We've never understood how big this library really is. We're dealing with over two thousand different interstellar species—just those who are registered. Plus the records of four thousand more who can't afford to join. Plus the records of several thousand *retired* species as well. The complete records of each and every one of those species—some of them with over a half-million years of recorded art and history and science—are stored in the InterChange. Everything they've ever seen or learned. Every planet they've ever visited, charted, explored.

"The library of the InterChange is so big and vast that not even the InterChange itself has any idea of how big it is. If we had started downloading the index to the index a hundred years ago, we still wouldn't even be half through! And that's an obsolete index! Sir, the InterChange is out of control. Nobody has a handle on its information anymore—not even the InterChange itself. The best that anyone can do now is dip into it like a mathematician browsing through the Mandelbrot."

The Ambassador blinked. "The Mandelbrot? That's an infinite object, isn't it? Surely, the InterChange can't be that vast—"

"It might as well be, sir. Even if we put a billion human beings on the job, our species still wouldn't live long enough even to catalog what's available, let alone download it. Do you see what I'm saying? There may or may not be an answer to any question you might possibly want to ask in the tanks of the InterChange—but there's no way anyone is ever going to locate it for you. It's lost in the stacks. The InterChange itself is lost in the stacks."

"But it works!" The Ambassador tried to protest. "The evidence is all around us—"

"No, sir. The evidence is all around us that the Inter-Change doesn't work. That's how the Rh/attes survive. They're information specialists. They find and identify the information that's immediately useful to a species. I don't know how they do it. If I did, we wouldn't need them, would we? The Rh/attes are the real InterChange here. They're providing the service! The InterChange can't.''

"You're saying that the InterChange is useless? Oh, my God.''

"Practically useless, sir. Those races who can afford the services of the InterChange know how futile it is; and those who don't know run up incredible debts in the process of discovery. And none of the member species wants to change the system, because they're afraid they'll end up worse off. It's the most incredible con game in the galaxy, because even the conmen who created it can't get out of it themselves anymore!''

The Ambassador sagged in his chair. His expression was stunned. "Then that means that . . . *everything* we've done here is wasted—Yake, I take it back. They're not going to hang you. They're going to hang me.'' He wiped his face with his handkerchief and looked up at Yake hopefully. "Is there anything else?''

"No, sir.''

The Ambassador sighed loudly. "I was hoping . . . against all hope, of course—that you might have found a direction. Do you think the Rh/attes can offer us any immediate help?''

"I don't know, sir. They don't offer information. You have to ask them the right question, and then be prepared to pay the price for the answer. They're very much like the Dragons that way. Cheaper, but still very enigmatic. I think, sir, that it's very much a matter of asking the right question. From the way that the Rh/attes have been acting, I'd guess that they know *something*—''

"I'm afraid to ask how much that something will cost.''

"Um. I probed, sir. They said what they say about all their answers. The information is valueless. It's what we might do with the information that creates value.''

"Yes.'' The Ambassador thought for a moment. "I tell you what. Let's start with a simple question.'' He reached across his desk for a folder marked EYES ONLY. "Here, try them on this. Ask them why this negotiation broke down.''

Yake took the folder. "Which one is this, sir?"

"The walking plants. The ones who were looking for a gardener. They spend the summer walking around, they put their roots down for the winter and meditate. They went into heavy debt to establish a colony on a new world, only to discover that there's some local predator that likes their flavor. It attacks them during their dream-time—peels back the leaves, scoops out and eats the living brains. These plant-creatures are conscious the whole time, but unable to do anything about it, so it's a very terrifying thing to them. They brought in another species, some kind of insect-race to help—the Ki!Lakken, they look like preying mantises—but they've totally failed to control these things.

"The contract looked like a natural for us; but when our people entered the room, the Fn^rr—that's what the plants call themselves—froze up and refused to talk. They curled their leaves in horror. And burned our negotiating team on the spot. We've filed a protest, of course—"

"Of course. Who was on the team?"

"Chandra. Hernandez. Bergman."

"Damn. They were good players."

"Save your grief. They were stupid. They went unarmed. We have a choice here, Yake. According to the rules of the InterChange, the Fn^rr have to pay us for the loss of our three negotiators, plus an insult fee. It's a pittance; it's worthless to us. *Or* . . . we can demand the satisfaction of a renegotiation. On our terms. I want to find out why they did it. That contract could have been useful. I think they were set up somehow—probably by the Dhroo."

"Why do you think that?" asked Yake. "It sounds right, but what evidence do you have?"

The Ambassador lifted a flimsy off his desk. He passed it over to Yake. "We've been served with a Notice of Acquisition. We have less than thirty days to demonstrate our intention to make good our information debt or the Dhrooughleem will take possession of us. For the record, the Dhroo have already worked sixteen species into early retirement. That's why I think the Dhroo are trying to kill our chances at any other deal—and if we can prove it, then we can file a grievance against the damn slugs. That will at least buy us some time. So. Do you think the Rh/attes can find ᷉ut anything here?''

"I dunno," admitted Yake. "But I'm willing to try it."

"Good. Just one suggestion.''

"Sir?''

"Make sure your team wears their sidearms from now on.''

"Yes, sir.''

THE
CHEESE
STANDS
ALONE

When Yake asked the question, the Rh/attes started giggling.

It was a particularly nasty sound.

Yake waited patiently for several moments, then spoke up with just the slightest hint of annoyance. "Are you going to let us in on the joke?"

"Joke, you are," replied the first Rh/atte.

The second Rh/atte added, "Vermin you call us; but vermin you are, too!"

The third Rh/atte wrung its bony fingers and pointed. "Gardeners the Fn^rr need to protect themselves. They see you; they see not the answer, but the problem!"

And all the Rh/attes started hissing and chittering together again. It was one of the finest jokes they had ever heard.

Yake turned around and looked at Nori and Madja and Anne, mystified. "Does anyone understand this?" They shook their heads.

"Missing a colony, are you?" the fourth Rh/atte asked. "Nineva Sector, perhaps?"

Yake looked to Kasahara. "Nori?"

Nori nodded. "Yes, but—that was over two hundred years ago. Long before we knew about the InterChange."

"Ahh . . ." said all the Rh/attes together.

"What was that?" asked Yake.

"That was answer expensive. Given freely," replied the fifth Rh/atte.

Yake wanted to glare at Nori, but held himself back. Instead he said, "Not given freely at all! We expect you to give us an answer of equal value."

The Rh/attes exchanged glances, then huddled together in conference to discuss that thought. Yake fumed.

127

Madja touched him on the shoulder then and he asked impatiently, "What is it?"

She whispered in his ear. "How do the Rh/attes know about our lost colony?"

Before Yake could answer her, the Rh/attes broke out of their huddle. The sixth Rh/atte spoke quietly. "This is why you are stupid, Earthman. There are only nine mammaloid species in the InterChange. The rest are equivalents of life forms you would call reptiles or insects or sea creatures. What is the difference most profound between mammals and the others?"

Yake shrugged. "We bear our young live. We suckle them. We care for them."

"Precisely. Mammaloid species raise their young. Other species not need to. Not on scale same. They reach adulthood quickly and without need for training and programming. They do not recognize mammaloids as capable of intelligence anyway. Why should they recognize what happens to mammaloid young when the young are not raised by parents? They see vermin. The Fn^rr see vermin. Who would see otherwise? Who would *know* otherwise?"

Yake was astonished. "Are you suggesting that there are— *feral* children out there? Human children?"

The Rh/atte paused and smiled. Its yellow teeth were long and sharp-looking. "I ask you question now, Earth-creature. Who finds planet for the Fn^rr?"

Yake looked to Nori. "Do we know that?"

Nori checked his clipboard. "Just a moment." His face froze as the answer came up on the screen. He held the screen for Yake and Madja and Anne to see.

Yake turned back to the Rh/atte. "The Dhrooughleem," he said quietly.

"Are you surprised?"

Yake ignored the question. His face had hardened into a mask of iron. "Isn't there some kind of rule in the Inter-Change against selling another species into slavery without an indenture?" he asked.

"Who is to know? Very shortly, who is to care? Slave now, slave then—all the same is."

Yake looked at his colleagues. They could all see the truth of that statement. Yake turned back to the Rh/attes. "Would you excuse us for a moment?"

THE
QUIET
ANGER

Madja was surprised to discover that Yake Singh Browne could out-swear her.

Yake could swear in English, Swahili, French, Russian, InterLingua, German, Italian, and Pascal. Yake could also break tables, chairs, lamps, and windows with surprising agility and strength.

Yake Singh Browne could go for fifteen minutes without repeating himself.

Afterwards:

They stood apart in the shambles of the room, exchanging glances. Yake was not ashamed to meet the others' eyes.

He said quietly, "I feel much better now, thank you. Shall we return?"

UNLOCKING
THE
KI!

When Yake returned to the room, the Rh/attes were still giggling among themselves.

He eyed them warily.

And then he made a mistake. He said, "There is more to this joke, I presume?"

They told him.

ANOTHER
GLASS
OF
BHEER

"The problem with bheer," said Yake to no one in particular, "is not that it doesn't taste like beer. It does. The problem is that it doesn't kick like beer."

"Yah," said Madja. "Is same problem with vhodka."

"And sahke," put in Kasahara.

"Ditto ghin," said Larson. "Alcoholh is not what it's cracked up to be."

"That is the problem," said Madja solemnly. "It's cracked from petroleumh—or is that petroleuhm? I forget which."

"It doesn't matter," said Yake. "The 'h' is silent."

"Ahh."

Nori looked up blearily. "Tell me again, Yake, is this really a good idea?"

"Nope," said Yake. "It's a really lousy idea. Getting drunk never solved anything. Getting dhrunk is even less of a solution."

"Then why are we doing it?" asked Larson, blinking and brushing her hair back out of her eyes.

"Because it was the *only* thing I could think of," Yake said. He opened another bottle. "Last time we got dhrunk, we had a ghood idea. I figured it might whork again—"

Madja blinked at that. "Last time we got dhrunk, you had to talk to Dragon. You want to do that again?"

Yake thought about that. Yake *tried* to think about that. "No," he said, finally. "Let's think of something else."

They thought in silence for a moment.

Abruptly, Yake looked over at Madja. She looked back at him. "Yes, what is it?"

"Do you wanna sleep with me tonight?"

"Is that all you think of?"

"No, but it's the only thing I can think of that I can do."

141

"I expect no less from capitalist swine," muttered Madja.

"Aww, don't be so hard on him. He's only a man." Larson said. "That's not his capitalism talking. That's his male chauvinism."

"No, no, no—it isn't *either* of those things," said Yake, slowly and carefully enunciating his words. "Everybody else in this InterChange is doing it to everybody else. I just wanna do it, too."

"That's lust," said Kasahara. "I know lust when I hear it."

"Yah," agreed Madja. "Sounds like lust to me."

"I doubt it," said Yake. "I think it's lhust."

"Is irrelevant," said Madja. "It brings us no closer to solution."

"I don't care anymore," said Yake. "I just wanna do it to somebody else for a change, instead of having it done to me."

"Yah," said Larson. "Me too."

"Me too," admitted Nori.

"I make it unanimous," added Madja. "Is galling to be treated like this."

Yake refilled his glass, held it up to the light, frowned and put it back on the table. Abruptly, he forgot about the bheer. "Hey—" he said, looking at the others. "What if there were a way to . . . do it?"

Madja returned his gaze. "If you find way, Yake—then you are better man than I. I sleep with you then."

"Hmm," said Larson. "Better be careful what you promise."

"I know what I promise. If Yake is that smart, then he is smart enough to be father of my children. Bring ring, Yake."

Yake grinned. "You got a deal, lady." He turned to Nori. "Turn on your magic clipboard and let's look at the rules of the game. You can't break 'em till you know what they are."

"Hey. Is no cheating allowed."

"Wrong, Madja—" Yake's grin was spreading from ear

to ear. "Is no playing fair allowed. In this game, it's how you cheat that counts!" Yake moved around the table to peer over Nori's shoulder. "Let's start by looking for loopholes—"

THE
SLIME
AND
THE
SMILE

Shuushulluu, the Dhrooughleem Ambassador, finished his ritual ablutions and slithered across the tank on his belly, his tentacles writhing in the slime. "Oh, great pool of life, I am yours to command. Touch me with your blessed wetness. I bring you tidings of great interest."

Lou'shloorloo the Wettest stroked one of Shuushulluu's tentacles dryly, and burbled, "Tell me what news transpires in the InterChange."

Shuushulluu glurped and replied, "The Terrans have refused our final offer, oh water of waters."

"Then the waters shall close over their heads. . . . On their own heads shall it be."

"Oh, my blessed rainfall—I wither before I contradict you; but no, the waters shall not close over their heads at all. They have found two service contracts for themselves."

Lou'shloorloo rose up in the tank, eyes blinking in wonderment and fear. "They have WHAT?"

"Oh, wetness—this so distresses me. I am salty with fear and embarrassment. We asked the Rh/attes to tell us who and how and what and why—but the Rh/attes are being paid to tell us nothing. Deliberately so! I fear for what this means! There are no clouds on our horizon! The dreadful sun beats down on us! Our waters boil and evaporate!"

The Dhrooughleem lord sank back into the tank. "We have promises to keep, my withering servant. You assured me that the naked Terran grubs would be ours by now to sell."

"I did not think—"

"That is apparent!"

"—that they could find an answer!"

"HOW DID THEY DO IT?"

147

"Then only thing that I can think, they must have seen the Dragon—"

"THEY CAN'T AFFORD TO ASK THE DRAGON!!"

"Then the only other possibility is that they were clever enough to negotiate a solution by themselves."

"YOU TOLD ME THEY WERE NOT THAT SMART!!"

"My lord, I have been proven terribly wrong. We had no evidence to suggest that any species derived from mammaloids could be capable of any real reasoning. It is common knowledge that mammalian creatures think with their glands. Now it seems that that common wisdom has been demonstrated wrong. I would wither and die for you."

"YOU DON'T GET OFF THAT EASY!! YOU AIR-SUCKING SCUM!!"

"Anything, oh anything—"

"TEN THOUSAND EGGS THIS WILL COST US!! AND THE OCEAN ONLY KNOWS HOW MANY MORE YEARS OF INDENTURE!!"

Shuushulluu flattened itself upon the bottom of the tank. "I am yours to command, oh blessed wetness—"

"HERE IS MY COMMAND!!"

"Yesss, oh very yesss!!"

"YOU WILL BE THE ONE TO TELL OUR OWN INDENTURER THAT WE WILL BE DEFAULTING ON THIS CYCLE. YOU WILL BE THE BEARER OF THE TIDE!"

"Oh, my blessed wetness—"

"BEGONE! GET THEE HENCE! YOU ARE FOULING MY TANK!!"

THE
WARM
LANDS

Again.
Again, the sun is warm, the leaves are bright.
Again, the blossoms grow.
The roots are warm. We walk again.
Anew. The world is new.
Again the dreams are true.
Anew.
The gardeners come. Come soon.
They have always been with us. Untrained. Unwise. They were as seedlings, always echoing, never knowing.
Echoing. Knowing.
Now, they shall be trained. And wise. So wise. They shall no longer eat the fruit of dreams.
The soil shall be warm. The blossoms will be bright. The seedlings soon grow tall and strong. The groves shall soon be large again.
Larger than a Fn^rr can walk within a season.
Again. Anew.
Soon, the gardeners live among us. The dreams of grubs and eaters in the orchards were seen through yester-season's eyes.
The eye of the sky shall smile. The rain will wash. The land will nourish. The soil will be rich.
The gardeners walk the dreams.
And the dreams no longer trouble.
Never again.
Again. Anew.
Again, tomorrow is found in dreams.
Again, we live anew.
Again.
Anew.

THE
CLACK
OF
THE
KI!LAKKEN

Hnaxx reached gingerly with one foreclaw and touched the bell that hung before the pavilion of the Egg-Master. A clear, sharp tone rang through the air. Hnaxx waited a respectful moment, then parted the silk hangings and entered.

The Egg-Master was waiting patiently on the High Dais. It was gently polishing its foreclaws with a silk. The Egg-Master had the most beautiful foreclaws; they were inlaid with precious metals and gemstones and polished to a high sheen.

After a moment, the Egg-Master looked up and seemed to notice Hnaxx for the first time. "Ah," it said. It put the cloth to one side and leaned forward intently. "You have news?"

"I have much news, my lord and Master. We shall be very prosperous indeed. Very prosperous. All has worked out quite well."

"Indeed?"

"Indeed. I shall endeavor to explain. You are acquainted with the offer made by the Dhroo?"

"The Dhroo were willing to sell us the grubs at ten sequins per unit; is this not correct?"

"Yes, my lord."

"Such a price seemed very high to all of us. Did it not seem high to you?"

"Yes it did, my lord. And there was that other matter, too. The one I shall not refer to after this."

"Yes, that other matter," said the Egg-Master.

"That one is now resolved as well. It seems, my lord, that we have been approached by another species—a mammalian one, if you can believe! They are called the Rh/attes and they are the representatives for the race of pale

155

grubs. Oh, you were right, my lord. These grubs are quite intelligent. The Rh/attes have been using them as slaves for years. We have been very fortunate in this matter. Now the Rh/attes will lease us individuals for only seven sequins per."

"There is a catch, I'm sure—"

"Oh, yes, my Master; there always is a catch; but this time, it is a catch that serves the buyer even better than the seller. They will only lease us individuals for one year at a time. But we can have as many as we wish. We may have hundreds. We may have thousands. We may have hundreds of thousands. We cannot use them for our breeding or our feeding, but we can use them any other way we want. We can train them, if we wish, to perform any tasks we choose, as long as we are not deliberately harmful. The Rh/attes will become our sole suppliers; they will take responsibility for every grub upon this world. But the chore of training, they insist, must be ours."

"For what we get, the price is still quite high."

"For what we get, the price is very low, my lord. We get a world free of Fn^rr. If I may be so blunt—these grubs will not need to be trained; all we have to do is set them free upon the land. They will figure out the rest themselves. They are predatory feeders. They will find the orchards and they will eat out the brains of the foolish Fn^rr while they sit and dream!"

"Your excitement," said the Egg-Master, "leads you to discourtesy, but in the face of such a bold arrangement, the enthusiasm you display might be called excusable."

"And once the Fn^rr are gone, the grubs will be ours to feed and breed upon. If the Rh/attes ask what has happened to their pets, we shall tell them that they died of a mysterious cause. We shall increase our numbers and the numbers of our nests. We shall retire many enemies! My Master, I am grateful to the nest that allowed me such an honor as this service."

"And the nest is grateful too, my child. You have served us well. We shall not forget what you have said and done. You shall be served in your time, too."

It wasn't until it was too late that Hnaxx realized exactly what the Egg-Master had promised.

THE
LAST
CARD
IS
TURNED

Yake, Madja, Anne, and Nori entered the room to applause. The Ambassador was standing at the head of the table, leading the hand-clapping.

They moved to their places at the table, smiling with good-natured embarrassment. Yake held up his hands to silence the acknowledgements of his colleagues. "Please," he said. "Please—not yet."

The applause continued for a few seconds longer, then died in uncertainty.

"Let me say this. It looks good. It looks very, very good. But we're going to have to wait to see if it plays. So please don't start slapping yourselves on the back and congratulating each other just yet. There's one more thing that has to happen, and I'm going to be taking care of it as soon as I finish my report here." He motioned to the others to sit down, but remained standing himself. "If you'll all be seated—"

Yake waited until everybody had taken their chairs and all eyes were upon him.

"It's very tricky," Yake began. "But it's all very, very legal. That's what's so delightful about it. First, the Dhrooughleem are out of the picture entirely. Because we found our own way of paying the debt, the Dhroo have had to forfeit a very large deposit that they paid to the Inter-Change for the right of sole acquisition. The deposit, I am told, was considerable—and part of it will be credited against our debt." Yake had to wait until the applause died down again before he could continue.

"Thank you. I feel that way myself. They bet the store and they lost it. But you don't know yet just how badly they lost it. The Dhroo were planning to sell human individuals to a race of intelligent praying mantises called the

161

Ki!Lakken: We got this information from the Rh/attes. This is what makes this game so interesting. The Dhroo thought that the Ki! wanted to use humans as food and as larval incubators. The Ki! were already using feral children for that purpose—'' Yake held up a hand. "I'll explain the details later; as near as we can figure out, these are the descendants of the lost Nineva colony. The Dhroo seem to have had a hand in that disaster, too.

"The thing is, some of the Ki! had figured out that the children could be trained, and they were planning to double-cross the Dhroo and the Fn^rr—" Yake paused. "This is about to get very complicated. The Ki! and the Fn^rr are sharing a planet—the same planet that the Dhroo stole from us. The Ki! wanted to purchase several hundred thousand humans, but not use them for food or incubators; they'd train them to kill the Fn^rr. Apparently the feral humans have been feeding on the Fn^rr. That would leave the Ki! the sole custodians of the planet. With the destruction of the Fn^rr, part of their debt would disappear. Is everybody following this? Good.

"So, we approached the Ki! with a better offer. Actually, we had the Rh/attes make the offer for us—for a small commission, of course. The Rh/attes will supply humans to the Ki! now. We'll get the fee, not the Dhroo. The contract specifically gives the Rh/attes, agenting for us, custody of all the humans on the planet. They can't be used for food or eggs; they can only be used for training. Nori Kasahara says that the Fifth, Seventh and Twelfth Armies can be briefed and on-site within seven months."

"But wait a minute—" said someone down at the end of the table. "That sounds like we're going to be a party to a genocide—"

"Oh yes, it does—doesn't it? But the contract is only for training; it guarantees nothing else. Of course, the Ki! don't dare say what they want to train the humans to do; that would be illegal."

"But we're not going to do it, are we?!!"

"Of course not. We have a second contract on that planet. We're going to be the new gardeners for the Fn^rr.

Caretakers. Protectors of the dreams. Call it what you will. It's a very attractive contract. Within ten years, the Fn^rr should have incredible forests on every continent.''

"But what about the Ki!? Won't they figure it out quickly enough?''

"Oh, I'm sure they will; but they're going to have some other problems to worry about. It seems that the Fn^rr have discovered a very interesting fact; the alternate larval beast that the Ki! use is very susceptible to the measles. To be very fair to our Ki!Lakken employers, we will have to make very, very sure that anyone sent to the planet is appropriately inoculated. Otherwise, it may turn out that the Ki!Lakken will not be able to continue into the next generation. And the Ki! have very short generations—only five to seven years.''

Yake let that sink in, then continued, ''So, here's how it works out. We're getting paid by the Ki! to eat the Fn^rr. We're getting paid by the Fn^rr to retard the breeding of the Ki!. If we decide to honor *both* those contracts, we can have our lost colony world back. We're getting part of the deposit forfeited by the Dhroo. Furthermore, because the Dhroo were responsible for stealing the planet from us in the first place and selling it to both the Fn^rr and the Ki!, they are heavily invested in both those species. Now that they've lost the rights to our indenture, they are no longer in a position to further exploit the Ki! and the Fn^rr, so they may not be able to meet the payments on their own indenture. So—if this forces an early retirement of the Dhroo, then the Rh/attes will pay us a bonus equal to one-tenth of *their* indenture to the Dhroo. Does everybody follow that?''

Everybody did. And this time, the applause went on and on and on.

Even after Yake left the room.

But there was still, as Yake had promised, one more thing to do.

ENDGAME

Yake Singh Browne had a promise to keep.

The Dragon was resting on the top of a brown hill. It looked up as Yake approached. It had been eating something wet and gray and slithery. Something that still bubbled and frothed. Pieces of glass and plastic crunched beneath its teeth; sea water dripped from its jaws. *"Yesss?"* it asked.

Yake bowed. "I came to keep a promise."

"You came to tell me how it all worked out?" the Dragon asked.

"Yes," said Yake. "I always keep my word."

"So. Now I will tell you," said the Dragon. *"It worked out deliciously. Thank you for an amusing game. I hope it was interesting for you."*

"Yes. It was very interesting. Very, very interesting."

"I am pleased. Perhaps you would like to play again soon?"

"Ah . . . if you insist." Yake sweated his answer. How do you say no to a Dragon?

"Yes, perhaps, we shall," said the Dragon. *"Perhaps next time it will be more interesting for me as well."*

The Dragon yawned and lowered its head to its feast again.

Yake ran like hell.

UNICORN & DRAGON

BY LYNN ABBEY

illustrated by
Robert Gould

A BYRON PREISS BOOK

An epic tale of two very different sisters caught in a fantastic web of intrigue and magic—equally beautiful, equally talented—charged with quests to challenge their power!

UNICORN & DRAGON *(volume I)*

75567-X/$3.50US/$4.50Can

"Lynn Abbey's finest novel to date"—*Janet Morris*
author of *Earth Dream*

AND IN TRADE PAPERBACK—

CONQUEST
Unicorn & Dragon, (volume II)

75354-5/$6.95US/$8.85Can

Their peaceful world shattered forever, the two sisters become pawns in the dangerous game of who shall rule next.